Four Queens

A Las Vegas Weekend

Carole Converse-Barnes

iUniverse, Inc.
Bloomington

Four Queens
A Las Vegas Weekend

iUniverse books may be ordered through booksellers or by contacting:

iUniverse
1663 Liberty Drive
Bloomington, IN 47403
www.iuniverse.com
1-800-Authors (1-800-288-4677)

ISBN: 978-1-4759-4717-5 (sc)
ISBN: 978-1-4759-4716-8 (hc)
ISBN: 978-1-4759-4718-2 (e)

Printed in the United States of America

iUniverse rev. date: 9/18/2012

Chapter One

A whisper of a breeze is moving the curtains from side to side as I mount Cowboy one more time before he leaves my bed. He will mysteriously disappear when he is sated, returning again when he feels the urge to join me for another few hours of shear ecstasy. I reach for his wet hair to bring him closer when the phone rings and I awaken from this wonderful dream with a start.

"Were you asleep Sissy?" Lucy's voice sings into the receiver.

"I was having sex," I joked, still wanting that dream back.

"Oh," she laughed, knowing I had no date mate and no batteries at the time. "I see. Let's get going to Las Vegas. I'm really looking forward to some quality time on the road."

I really don't want to get up, I want to keep dreaming. Normally I lie in bed and think of all the unremarkable things I've done in life knowing once those thoughts are finished the day will only get better. Low expectations are so much easier to achieve and there is seldom disappointment when the bar is low.

My name is Sissy French and I'm an incurable romantic. More than a few of my waking hours are spent fantasizing about a perfect relationship with a perfect man. An oxymoron perhaps, but in life there is always hope. The ideal mate concept, although unrealistic, fills a void that would otherwise be dreary reality.

Lucy is my number one friend, possibly because she looks like she is channeling Lucille Ball without even trying. Her mannerisms are similar, but with a 2012 twist. Some nights she pulls her bright red hair up to be captured in a triangular checkered scarf which she ties in front in the same fashion as Lucille Ball. It is impossible to describe the humor to people who are not familiar with the antics of Lucille Ball.

I cherish all time spent with my two best friends and I'm restless to head out on our short road trip to Las Vegas.

"Sometimes it seems like too much trouble to have sex," I laughed. My previous two romantic episodes could best be categorized under the heading crime and punishment. "We aren't leaving for several days. What are you doing?"

"Remember our discussion relating to the abused women? I am jumping into the project. I have been planning all morning and I've had far too much caffeine."

"What time is it? My clock must have stopped. It says seven o'clock. How long have you been up?" I asked.

"It's early, but I couldn't sleep so I just decided to set up a timetable for the project before we lost interest."

"O.K. just let me get beautiful, or just presentable, and I'll see you at Doug's café, (a sandy beach café with too much sand on the floor), in about forty five minutes."

We had met the previous day for lunch and then afterwards headed over to Lucy's to watch old movies, sip some Late Harvest Riesling, and try on old clothes that were barely used and clearly no longer fit our profiles. Our brilliant plan was to create a collection center for women's clothing and then donate the proceeds to a neighborhood shelter for abused women. We felt our project should take at least a week to organize, after which we would hit the road for a little rest and relaxation in Las Vegas. We were determined to finish this project, unlike several other well intentioned efforts in the past that had never actually materialized due to unexpected sidetracks or lapses in enthusiasm.

I looked down at my white legs. It was Halloween season, but that was no excuse. It was time for the bronzer, but maybe not this morning. There were people who could successfully apply bronzer without having dark knees and feet, but I was not one of them. I could apply it on others perfectly, but on me, no chance.

I agonized as I crawled out of my cozy shopping channel flannels and looked for the remote control so I could have the television on while I started the morning ritual. I had years of devilish behavior behind me, so Sundays were now a time to listen to a couple of favorite religious speakers and contemplate redemption.

My friends and I are at a happy place. There is not a cougar among us. We look at men the same age or older hoping they know who Van Morrison and Bob Dylan are and wouldn't expect us to remain forty forever. It seems very unsettling to each of us to want to keep up with a younger man. We keep our prospective lovers older, wiser, wealthy, and of course, clever, distinguished and sexy. None of us are lacking notches on our bracelets.

My newly pedicured feet hit the cold tile as I sneak up on the mirror hoping to see a face ready to leave the house, but that was not the case this morning. This face needed work, and the hair, OMG, (meaning Oh My Goodness, not Obama Must Go as was a bumper sticker I saw earlier in the week) had a kind of orangutan do, with a noticeable grow out. I needed to start the electric rollers or there would be no leaving the house today. Dark blonde was my color of choice, not too different from my natural shade, but just light enough to show one month's roots.

The phone rang again between eyeliner and lash application, screwing up my left eye as I blinked in surprise.

"Yes?" I said with some stinging in the damaged eye.

"Are you almost ready?" Lucy asked. "Should I call Mattie to have her meet us?"

"Please do, I am almost ready to meet the day." I reached for the make-up remover and the Visine for my now reddening eye.

Lucy phoned Mattie asking her to meet for breakfast so we could get our timeline finalized for the project. Mattie was always ready regardless of the time she got up. She just looked good in bed hair and no make-up. She was really quite fabulous any time any way. She had a natural tan year round. Mattie refused to make a lot of facial expressions for fear of future wrinkles and wouldn't even use straws for fear of mouth lines. We mused that she resembled a blond Jack in Box clown. She was as genuine as a person could be and without pretense. She had a heart of gold and gave to all animal charities even fostering animals herself much of the year.

"Nice to see you this morning," Lucy said, as I walked into the breakfast bar.

"Yes, and always nice to see you my lovely friend," I said with some stinging still in one eye.

"I spoke with Mattie," she said, "she will be here shortly."

We were looking forward to this project whole heartedly, but we also were looking forward to a short trip to Las Vegas for a few days of shopping and sun soaking. Sun soaking as we defined it included being under a cabana with forty-five SPF sun screen covering our bodies.

Gathering slightly used clothing from women around the immediate neighborhood was our primary target for the donation. Women, including the three of us, keep stuffing clothing into closets until it becomes necessary to buy armoires to hang new garments. We hoped to capture these similar mentalities with our plea to part with clothing they had not seen for some time. Seeing our colorful flyers in store windows might help stimulate a desire to part with some of last decade's clothing. Even in San Diego with the fabulous weather we still have seasonal changes. Donating was good for the soul. *Cleanse your soul by giving to the less fortunate,* that wording would start our flyers in hopes it would reach the generation who knew what a soul was and not the new soulless generation roaming the world.

Mattie arrived in hat, long white tee, leggings and red framed sunglasses, and the three of us ordered a small breakfast and began finalizing our thoughts for the project.

We agreed on our timeline and planned to draw up graphics on the computer that day, run the colored flyers around the neighborhood and place them at all the boutiques we could talk into giving us the space. We thought a week should be plenty of time to collect the donations, get them separated, and delivered. Five dollar Starbucks' certificates would be given to anyone bringing more than five outfits.

We would deliver the donated items to an address received from a friend in the police department. The address was confidential, not unlike witness protection safe houses.

We spent four hours that afternoon talking with understanding shop owners and placing the flyers. By Wednesday donations started piling up at the stores and store owners called to have us come and get bags that were "in the way". A quick tally of the donations showed we needed thirty Starbuck certificates for the women who had left names and addresses and a minimum of five items. Quite a haul!

We proudly continued to gather the bags from different locations for the balance of the week and began sorting through bras, panties, skirts, sweaters and blouses. There were cosmetics and facial products also that the girls would find useful and fun.

"Oh My God, look, evening gowns! What generous person felt an abused woman would be looking for a cocktail dress, a slutty cocktail dress, when she got back on her feet and hit the job market?" I laughed.

There were five gowns all together, but no name for a certificate. We could see why! They were rather whorish in cut and color and the slinky fabric stretched the imagination as to where they had been. We just couldn't give these to the shelter. Instead, the bag would go into the trunk and at some point hopefully be of service to some very special recipients.

Las Vegas, the destination for our long weekend away, was getting closer. I personally never liked the desert and I couldn't understand why people liked living in the center of dusty gray land with rocks for landscaping and cactus for color. Succulents were popular, possibly a fad, in San Diego, but they were complimented by ample flowers and trees. For a true vacation I needed resort living with golf courses and tropical weather not dust, sand fleas and dry skin. After moving to San Diego from the rainy northwest there was little need to travel very far for better weather, just a change of activities periodically.

However, we all like to gamble. We love the silicone and make-up and big hair. Shopping in Las Vegas is a draw for all three of us.

Lucy and Mattie longed to dress and dine in something other than jeans and although none of us would be seeing forty again we looked far better than most in their thirties and we love the attention all women appreciate when men spin their heads to watch as we walk by.

And of course there are the magnificent casino interiors that kept me in awe. The complexity and creativity in the design of new casinos is always over the top. The imagination behind the selection of the interior colors and finishes always sends my mind reeling. Often I thought of working on a casino project, but just could not force myself to live in Las Vegas. So I traveled there a couple of times a year to buy a few new items and explore the new casinos and as an added bonus explore the new design center on the Northwest side of the city. Visiting the design center for a week could not make a dent in my investigating the hundreds of showrooms, but always I have a great time trying.

Las Vegas is where we were going and we were determined to have a rollicking good time, a girl time, with no precise return time planned. We cleared all appointments for the next five days and notified our clients that we would call them when we returned. Design, real estate, dance, and tattoo kept us quite busy. Our clients would wait. None of us had the nine to five burden suffered by most. Lucy's house had the esthetician station and my home housed the real estate office/ design office. Earlier in life we found that having licenses for everything that interested us would prove a very wise decision, not only for discounts but allowing us to create our own comfortable work hours. We had all endured years of corporate bullshit from near psychotic micro managers.

Over the weekend we poured through the donations, separating by colors, fabrics, styles and functions. Our flyers had produced a tremendous response and we estimated we had acquired over four hundred pounds of dresses, skirts, coats, jackets, shoes, hats, purses and other useful items. Virtually all the donations we had collected were in pristine condition, which was a truly pleasant surprise.

By Monday morning we had packed the car to over flowing with bags of donations and we were excited to pass along the product of our labor. We drove until we found the location of the women's shelter and rang the bell on the back door. Our instructions were very specific about not using the front door. There was a long driveway and a garage at the end of the property and we were directed to park there and quickly honk the car horn twice. Someone from the house would then observe our license plate and come out to help us with the bags.

"Let's not take those horrid evening gowns in. We can probably dispose of them in Las Vegas. Maybe we can give them to an Elvis Chapel."

"That sounds like a good idea," I said and so the gowns were left in the car, none of us realizing how fate would later reward us for that impromptu decision.

I felt both sorrow and compassion for these women, knowing that full time security is required to keep them healthy and alive. There is a wonderful network created in the county for those who had gotten away from abusive homes and now were living by themselves on an income they were proud to bring home.

We entered the house and looked around the basic kitchen, seeing several women at the stove and others preparing food to cook for an evening meal. They all looked out of place in that colorless, institutional kitchen and you knew that their own kitchens at home were much different, or at least more personal. Living here was like camping out.

Later that evening the boxes and bags of clothes would be unpacked allowing the women to try on garments and choose items for themselves that would be appropriate when they found new jobs. We all watched the bags being brought through the door and placed beside a mountain of other wonderful donations. There would be a great deal to choose from later this evening for this group of abused women. There were a staggering number of women who came through the center's doors everyday.

This particular center, being one of the larger, had a volunteer staff of professionals that came weekly, donating their time, giving make-up lessons, business classes, psychological reviews, money management classes and many other personal programs to the women who needed the services. There was a great deal of work involved in running this home for women of so many nationalities and upbringings. Some of the women were divorced, or without an education, or beaten, without a sense of self, pregnant without a husband or support of any kind. Runaways came here seeking shelter from the violence on the streets. Educated women, whose husbands had left taking everything including the secretary, came for comfort and training to get back to a life they could live by themselves.

One woman who sat on a stool in the kitchen with a glass of iced tea, smiled as we glanced her way. She was quite beautiful, very tall and Jamaican I guessed. She had a black eye and bruised cheek. Her long sleeves, on a hot day like today, made me think her arms may be bruised also.

I walked over to her. "Hi," I said. "I'm Sissy."

"I'm Boo," She said.

"Boo? That's very cute."

"Yes, my husband always called me Boo-who after he hit me and I kind of liked the name so it stayed with me. This is not my first time here, but I hope it will be my last."

"I love your positive attitude." I went over to shake her hand which she extended to me.

"Will you be staying here much longer? Do you have a job in place after you leave?"

"I may be here for one more day, but I think that will be long enough. I came last night. My husband usually leaves for a hunting trip with the boys after something like this happens."

She was very pretty with a wide smile and I wanted her to be my friend. It felt invigorating to have her in my personal space. I wondered if we could keep in touch after she went home.

I looked at Mattie and Lucy who were mingling with the girls and having coffee. I motioned to them and asked if they would come over and meet Boo. They were happy to oblige and easily made conversation with her about her situation. Boo was very open about her life and kept the conversation upbeat. I needed to move the car from the driveway to let in another vehicle so we excused ourselves with gentle hugs all around.

"I thought we could take Boo with us to Las Vegas," I said as we went to see if all the clothes were out of the car and move it over. They looked startled that I would want to do that, not knowing a thing about her, but they found no reason to object. "I thought it would give us a new friend and a new life to talk about as we travel through the desert on I-15."

Mattie and Lucy were in agreement that Boo might make a great travelling companion. I went back to where she was seated and explained that we had a room and show reservations in Las Vegas the coming weekend and invited her to join us.

"Just some money for food when we stop should take care of it," I said.

"That will be the best chapter in my life so far," Boo said. "I am not here because I have no money. I'm here because I do not wish to be found and Gladys is used to seeing me here every three or four months. I always pay to be here and help the others with some personal items. I won't be going through this again. My life will take a new direction when I leave here, of that I am certain."

We exchanged phone numbers and I turned to leave.

So now we had four people and no room to spread out in our car. We would make something work though, we always did.

"Sissy," Boo said. "I have an SUV with a small trailer. It has a cover, and it is at our disposal," she laughed a little, "if you would like. I am the registered owner so there's no problem with our taking it."

Lucy and Mattie and I were like small children when we heard her offer the car. We could actually spread out and put our luggage in the trailer while we were traveling. What a luxury. We are all bad travelers suffering from PADD, (packing attention deficit disorder). To further aggravate that situation no one wanted to drive longer than an hour and we had to stop at all malls and restrooms. That was SADD, (short attention driving disorder).

"We may go further than Las Vegas if we are traveling in comfort," Lucy said. Smiling in contentment at one another we left the center anxiously looking forward to the coming Thursday when we would hit the road with our new friend.

I looked back as we left and Boo was beaming radiantly in the sunny window. She looked like a cat taking in the heat of the sun and I felt sorry for her husband. He could not replace her very easily. I hoped I would meet him one day if only to tell him so.

There was no limit to what we could take now; additional hair, make-up, shoes, and electric rollers. Simply put, everything we were previously going to cut back on to save space.

We would also take the bag of evening clothes, just in case we saw some women who might look good in those whorish garments. Perhaps some shelter in Las Vegas could use them to help a few special women get back to work.

"Let's put those glorious evening duds in a garbage sack and use it in the back of her SUV for a pillow," I said to Mattie. "I think we will love our new friend, don't you? She needs us you know."

"I think we should let her know where we will be staying, what shows we will be seeing and what our planned activities include so that she will have an idea of what clothes might be fun to take," Lucy said.

Two days passed and I called Boo on her home phone. She seemed very happy and asked that we stop by and have some wine that evening with her at her home. I was anxious to get to know more about Boo. She gave me easy driving directions so I phoned Lucy and Mattie asking them to be ready at five o'clock.

Mattie ran into Costco while Lucy double parked and picked up some sushi. Blocks before we arrived we noticed how the land opened up and each home faced the ocean with a large lot on the entry side. There were no apartments just rather nice fenced custom homes designed to be unique and not resemble the neighbor's property.

Boo had a multitude of flowers in the front yard, some rather wild, but so many colors that you felt you might be in the middle of the Carlsbad flower fields. We did not see any people at home next door but we heard the sound of what might have been a peacock and crashing waves. A broken glass top, perhaps from a cocktail table, was by the front curb for pick-up. I thought it must have been part of Boo's fight with Joe.

I rang the bell and Boo answered in jeans and a white sweater. With her beautiful mocha skin she looked pretty outstanding. She really could get by with just this ensemble in Las Vegas.

"Come in," she said with a smile in her voice as if we had been friends forever. "Come this way to my favorite room and we can avoid the mess in the living room."

I believed if you followed God's lead he would show you the best in friends and in life and Boo was going to be one.

Lucy immediately walked to the figurines, some of which had been glued back together, and fondled them as if they were her own.

"These are beautiful," Lucy said. "Some are very old aren't they?"

Lucy had made pottery all of her life and finer porcelains were always a treasure for her. She owned the kilns and the slip and the forms to pour almost anything. After her divorce Lucy had more time to apply her pottery skills, which pleased her to no end. Her settlement kept her in the same house and actually nothing in her life changed except her trying to please the ex. They even used the same attorney and were able to talk on the phone like friends after a short time. It was a divorce made in heaven. Lucy had her 34 A-cup boobs upsized to 34 C-cup immediately after the divorce papers were signed, something her ex-husband would never allow.

"Many of the figurines have been broken and repaired," Boo said. "Joe always knew what would hurt me the most. Many were my Mom's and some were gifts from previous men friends. He never broke what he had given me which, in retrospect, was not that much." Boo shook her head and sighed.

I admired the way she spoke of him in past tense and hoped she was free of him forever. Her brightly colored furniture was fabulously overstuffed. We sank into the down cushions and felt very much at home. I saw pictures of Joe on the fireplace and thought he was a decent looking man, and I could see being drawn to him in a bar or store or on vacation. In another picture they were standing side by side and I noticed she was quite a bit taller than him. Some men did not like that I thought to myself and as if reading my mind, Boo started talking about him.

"He hates my being taller. My wearing heels or tall hair just makes him livid. But that started after several years, not at first, but as time went on," Boo said shrugging her shoulders.

Several pictures of Joe were with other men, whom I assumed were the ones he was away with now. Some Mexican, some Puerto

Rican, they all looked like they preferred roughing it to living indoors. They were probably joking about Boo's treatment and how she will be glad to have Joe home. He is a son of a bitch for hurting her and I hoped he would get hurt in some fashion.

"Are you going to move furniture and clothes out before he comes back?" I asked as I headed for the wine.

"No, my brother and his friend will do all that is necessary the afternoon we leave," Boo said, as she loaded a plate with sushi.

She said her brother would not say a word about her and Joe's behavior to anyone. He is always her closest confident when anything is wrong in her life. Her brother would have killed Joe if he had known where her many trips away had taken her. She did not share Joe's abusive nature with her family. Her mother never spoke of her father's abuse and she thought probably her grandmother did not speak of her abuse either.

The four of us were a good fit. We all had stories of past failures and wondered if brain scans or shock therapy might have helped. We laughed and talked about our past relationships finding our own stories hard to believe.

I couldn't wait to share more successes and failures on the trip. Time would go too fast, but we did have the rest of our lives.

We wanted to help Boo pack dishes or something that night, but she refused saying this is no one's fault but her own and she is certain there wasn't enough that her brother couldn't get it done.

After leaving Boo that night we all agreed that finding her at the shelter and having her come with us will make a great trip even better.

True to her word, Boo was at my house at 8:00 am Thursday morning. The SUV with a darling eight foot trailer attached was clean and sparkling in the morning sun. There was more than ample room for luggage. There was a separate locked tool box the width of the trailer in shining chrome.

"I own some fabulous china and crystal that I wrapped after you left. I did not want to bother you to help and as you see it isn't that much. It will be safe in there," Boo said. "I will keep it locked."

Boo told me the trailer was made for a beautiful dog, her special pet. Joe let it out on purpose and it was hit by a passing vehicle in front of their house. Boo raced it to the closest animal hospital, but it did not survive and her hatred for Joe grew more intense from that day forth. After that tragedy she no longer prepared meals or cleaned the house regularly. She showed little attention to Joe and tried to make every part of his life as hellish as possible. There are so many things to find out about Boo I could hardly wait.

"Your home is lovely," she said. "I love the pinks and reds blended together."

"I love color. I met Lucy when we both did major design projects in the city. Our tastes were similar and we decided to do residential projects together on the side, not compromising our regular commercial design jobs. My style is kind of "my client changed their mind and won't pay". Luckily, great furniture can usually be reupholstered to accommodate the end user. This is my pink, red and white period. I will change in another year, but right now I feel very good with this theme. I adore Tiffany lamps, so I matched the color palette in the lamps to the rest of the room decor. It works well and at night it creates a Las Vegas look thankfully lacking the aggravating noise and smoke."

"I'm missing an animal companion right now. I'm seriously thinking about adopting a puppy from the local shelter when we get back from Vegas and giving them a pink or red animal bed!"

I had one large purple suitcase filled to the brim and my electric rollers that would be placed in the trailer. My makeup/jewelry bag I would keep in the Escalade. Everything was perfect so far and we had tons of space to bring back all sorts of fabulous purchases from Vegas.

Next we went to Mattie's home which was actually a second story downtown condo featuring a panoramic view of the San Diego skyline and the Pacific Ocean. Parking in front was short term only so we both ran up the stairs to get Mattie and her luggage.

The door was open and she was watering her house plants, placing them all on one table in the dining room so the cat sitter could easily keep them watered. Mattie's condo had a fabulous contemporary interior all done in white and green. Everything was upholstered in chenille or leather. Green sheepskin area rugs were placed over the bleached hardwood floors. Outside the bedroom door a long haired white cat was nestled down on a green rug cleaning her paws and waiting to have the space all to her own.

Two Eames chairs faced the view and all the art was large, framed and triple matted in blacks and moirés. Mostly Erte, but many artists from the deco period graced her silk walls. I always hated leaving her condo when my visit was over.

Mattie also had one large suitcase and her jewelry and make-up bag so we were still looking good on the baggage space available.

We flew down the stairs just as the meter maid came to the truck. We begged her to let us go in happiness and not have to pay that twenty-five dollar ticket. She was just starting to write our ticket and we all looked hopelessly pitiful as she tore out the ticket and handed it to Mattie. "Have a great morning," she said with a smile. Mattie blessed her and we were gone in an instant, now on our way to Lucy's house for the final pick-up.

Boo asked if we minded stopping for a Starbucks after picking up Lucy so that we would be wide awake for the trip. I could hardly wait. Hot chocolate soy, extra grand size with extra chocolate is my favorite drink in the world. It is my only sugar intake so I always order the largest size available knowing that is all the sugar I can have for an entire day. Having gone through cancer twice I knew sugar to be a major taboo and I hoped that I had told enough people over the past years about the sugar/cancer relationship.

Lucy's home was located in a gated community with a security gate that had to be navigated in order to gain entrance. We arrived fifteen minutes later after going thru a minor traffic hold up. I had the code for the gate so in we went. The grounds were always kept like Augusta Golf Course, without a weed or cigarette butt in sight.

Lucy was taking out the garbage. It was in sacks so that the large green container would not be sitting on the curb or blown away in the Santa Ana winds that were predicted to hit the day after we left.

Her yard, beautifully landscaped with a small pool and gorgeous flowering plants in very colorful ceramic pots from Mexico, looked like a Kincaid year round. Up lighting situated under most of the plants made it sparkle like fireflies at night from the large windows in the living area. She is a natural horticulturist and it seemed everything grew and flourished when planted. There was also a community pool maintenance man who was very exciting to look at when he cleaned the pool. He provided great fantasy material throughout the years. Lucy had also turned her art studio into a guest cottage and moved her kilns and pottery into the house after her divorce just to be closer to her art. She loved having company there to stay.

The inside of the home was done very eclectic with colors in the purple/turquoise/green family. She clearly had wonderful taste in furniture and art and still attended architecture classes on design long after her career as a commercial designer ended. We had taken many trips to the furniture markets in High Point, North Carolina and were now were blessed with the Las Vegas World Design Center. We still went to High Point if we wanted a golf destination because golfing there was fabulous and less expensive than Las Vegas.

We put Lucy's two pieces of luggage in the trailer and away we went. We still had plenty of room in the trailer for shopping items and lots of space to stretch out in the SUV. Lucy thoughtfully brought neck pillows for all of us and a couple of light blankets. There was a cooler with water and juice, some protein bars and of course our gin soaked yellow raisins for health. We were ready for our Starbucks' caffeine rush.

As we entered Starbucks a large pock faced man with huge sweat circles on his red shirt rushed passed us, jostling Lucy and practically knocking her down.

"That's a rude son of a bitch," Boo said. The big man obviously heard the comment and turned to give her a look that would have frightened someone more timid, but she turned to confront him and said "yes, you."

His face, flushed and sweaty, indicated he was clearly riled. He walked towards her as we protectively scurried to her side, and said,

"Keep your mouth shut bitch and you will live longer." With that expletive he turned, strode to the curb, and slid into the front seat of a large white Sprinter van already occupied by two other passengers. With a gnashing of gears and a loud gunning of the engine the van dramatically exited the parking area.

"Well, this is an interesting start to a week of fun and games. As vacations go, I'd say about an eight. Other than his sweat stains, he seemed to have some major problems that he really wanted to share with us," said Mattie, laughing as she headed for the colorful coffee mugs on display. I knew she would buy one. It was just Mattie. In fact, we had never been to an event that didn't provide a new cup for home.

"I didn't like the look in that man's eyes. I wonder what that facial tattoo looked like before all the lines and scar tissue appeared on his cheek. I strongly suspect he will hurt someone before this day is over," said Boo.

"What is your drink of choice girls?" said a preppy voice from the attractive young barista behind the counter. His name tag revealed we were about to be served by "Troy" and we noticed behind his shoulder was his photo entitled employee of the month.

"We are an easy lot, young man. We would like four hot chocolates with soy, extra chocolate please, extra large size, no whipping cream," I said, speaking for all of us.

"Yes ladies," he said with a cute, college boy smile.

While watching young Troy prepare our libations my mind drifted off a bit, remembering what sweet sixteen (possibly sweet fifteen) years old was like. Oh yes. Those were the back seat days, the rushing hormones, the falsies, the skimpy underwear and under wire bras ordered from a Victoria's Secret catalog. Hours spent scouting for those wonderful colognes in your best friends' mother's bedroom; scents that seemed to last for days. All of those half truths you told your mom so you could spend time with unruly off limit boys. Oh yes, I remembered all too well.

"Did you notice that sponge faced man who just left in such a hurry? He almost knocked us over," I said.

"Yes, he was not a pleasant man and I was particularly careful not to serve him the wrong beverage. He paid with a hundred dollar bill and his look dared me not to have change. Fortunately, the night deposit had not been made this morning and I grasped that money like it was all my own. Maybe he didn't like getting up this early! I'm always thankful that we have the cameras going so if someone kills me, the police can at least have a look at the offender."

We laughed, hoping he was kidding because he looked like someone that would be missed by many hot girls.

"Where are you ladies going this early?"

"We need to gamble, dress up, stay out late, and act immature for a few days," Mattie said, offering him a big smile.

"Wish I was going. You four look like more fun than I have ever had!" He said.

"Or ever will," we almost said in unison.

We snickered and gave him a big tip before going to the truck and organizing ourselves for the next leg of our journey.

We had some big pillows behind the back seat and our garbage bag of evening clothes, so we put those in the areas where we thought we would be lounging.

"This is magnificent! We can trade front seat position when anyone wants. I have more space than I know what to do with," Lucy said impishly. "It's nice to have the extra trailer space."

"Every time I think I should sell the trailer, a good idea comes to me and I keep it a little longer," Boo smiled. "I think after this trip I will sell it."

We all wore loose clothes to avoid those dreaded yeast infections and idle leg blood clot possibilities. All of those years of looking good for someone else were behind us. We had a more common sense approach now; comfort first, cute second.

We slowed for a yellow signal light at the last intersection before entering the freeway north and then pulled to a stop as it turned red. We heard the horn on the vehicle behind us as it screeched to a halt, the driver probably thinking we should have gone through.

After driving in California for only one month I realized you never leave room in front of your car regardless how fast you are

Four Queens

going, you do not use your blinker and you never stop for yellow or red lights without the person behind you blasting the horn. We turned to look and were shocked to see it was the horrible big red skinned man from the coffee shop. He shook his fist at us while one of his buddies gave us the finger.

"Now isn't that the same unpleasant fellow from before? I'd assumed we wouldn't encounter his bad ass again in this lifetime, but here he is. I hope the light changes soon so he doesn't come up here," I said.

"Let's remember we have a couple of guns with us and spray cologne. I would prefer to use the gun and not waste my Angel perfume, but nothing will prevent me from showing him I know how to use either if he ventures this way," Boo said. "Can you imagine him smelling like an Angel?"

Fortunately the light turned green and we were once again on our way, towing our little trailer and feeling relatively safe and secure with our big SUV and our little guns.

Chapter Three

Boo wanted to talk about Joe as our trip began. That was great. We all wanted to know how he turned out to be such a cruel and uncaring bastard.

Boo said she had met Joe in Cuba on the dock where he was getting ready to go marlin fishing out of her parent's charter company. Her mother introduced them.

She was accustomed to making the acquaintance of the charter clients, but he seemed special, someone she would like to spend more than just bait time with. He had a way with her mother that was rather charming.

She described him as having wavy brown hair and being her height when she wore flats. She'd seen him in shorts and a blue tee that showed his muscular arms and very even tan and she loved the way he cajoled all the older people around him.

As the boat pulled away from the dock he whistled to get her attention and she turned right away. She scolded herself afterwards, but secretly relished the attention and felt good about it inside.

As the boat departed the dock she watched from the window of the bait house waiting to see if he would turn to look for her and much to her satisfaction he did.

A half hour after the boat had returned to the dock that evening there was a knock on her door. There he was, a white cotton shirt, opened half way down his chest, beige linen trousers, some black rubber flip flops and a hand full of flowers in one hand. In the other hand he dangled a tilapia fish hanging from a line. He looked good.

He said the fish was for her mom, the flowers for her. Or if he thought he would be a bigger hit, Boo could have the fish and her mom the flowers.

She told him the flowers would smell better in her room than the fish. I laughed while she was taking a breath and enjoying the hot chocolate.

He told her he was there for a week and then he was back to San Diego where he had an import/export company. He actually had no product inventory stored in warehouses; he simply ordered and sold on line so he had no overhead or middleman expenses other than a computer.

He said he liked to fish and had several buddies in the area where he lived that he often camped and vacationed with, but this week was different. This week was supposed to be a real vacation, away from all his friends and usual activities. He really poured on the charm when he mentioned that meeting her confirmed he had made an excellent decision.

Joe wanted to sample some of the local color, so after a few drinks at Raul's Tiki Bar Joe suggested they dine at The Harbour Club, a private club for mostly white business men in downtown Havana where Hemingway had often hung out, back in the day. Beautiful senorita hostesses circulated the dining area but Joe assured Boo she was by far the most attractive woman there and she fell for it, hook, line and sinker.

She had never thought of leaving Cuba until that very moment.

Joe lived on the water in San Diego and spent a great deal of time away from home. It sounded good, almost magical.

The week with Joe was a special time for Boo. He paid a great deal of attention to her and hung around her folks as if they were family.

She once saw him talking to some young girls on the corner in Havana while she shopped. He seemed to have a special talent for speaking to total strangers, a natural charisma. The girls seemed totally absorbed in what he was saying and they gave him a card before leaving him. She never brought it up.

The day he departed she took him to the airport but he surprised her by jumping out at the curb before she could park the car and go in the terminal to kiss him good-bye. She thought that was rather odd, but they had exchanged kisses and hugs before getting into the car so maybe Joe was just in a hurry.

He said he hoped to hear from her soon and would send her an open ended plane ticket if she wanted to visit him in San Diego. If she used it he would be very happy.

Her mother and father were surprised later that month when she decided to use the ticket, but they were not really unhappy with the decision. She had been with them since birth and she was thirty.

After she arrived in San Diego, Joe and his friends would go to factories and businesses to see product, so they had several trips a year away from home. Sometimes he would come home in very good spirits and sometimes he would be unbearable. He would say he had people problems when he came home in an angry state and in a day or two he would improve his mood and become loving and charming once again.

The sex was always good, there were no serious fights, and one year later he asked her to marry him. She looked forward to a family of her own and eagerly accepted his proposal. They agreed that the wedding ceremony would be low key and very small, but the weekend they were to be married Joe had an emergency trip out of town. Her parents were coming and Boo was pissed.

That was the first time she raised her voice to Joe and said he reeled back a bit and snapped back at her in an angry tone.

Pre-wedding jitters she thought. She notified the guests and the wives and girlfriends of Joe's friends and they did not seem all that surprised. Joe had postponed or cancelled a lot of events over the years they told her.

The day of the wedding arrived and Joe had gotten home late the night before. He was tired and his hands showed mysterious scrapes and bruises. Boo questioned Joe about his condition and he explained that he had fallen at the airport departure gate in his haste to get home to her. He said he scraped his hands on the cement trying to break his fall.

Boo told us the wedding was a pleasant affair and everyone seemed to enjoy themselves, but Joe's friends were in a lot of private conversations after the ceremony, which seemed a bit odd. Nevertheless, the mood was upbeat and, at Joe's suggestion, they headed off for a honeymoon in Panama City, a place Joe had often referred to as a "colorful jewel".

Boo said Joe told her she would love the country. The people were very congenial, the views are beautiful and the property is like Hawaii used to be fifteen years ago. They should buy a house there while the prices were low he said.

Panama turned out to be a very beautiful place, just as Joe had said. He had a few meetings set up there with manufacturers of products he said he wanted to start carrying, but if they had time, he wanted to fly to Mexico City and call on some clients there also. It was up to Boo if she wanted to go there with him he told her. He would come back home if she wasn't game.

She told him she'd love to go. She had never been to Mexico City. She could buy art and pottery and have it shipped to the house.

She suggested to Joe that he find a good pottery manufacturer and perhaps bring that into his lines. He laughed at her.

She spent most of each day by herself shopping for items to send home. She would only be there three days. Joe would join her in the evening for dinner and a swim. Then he would go to bed, exhausted from his business ordeals of the day.

The day they were leaving the phone rang and a man asked if Joe was there. Boo said no, but he would return shortly, and asked if there was a message. She thought that was a normal request from a wife.

The man on the phone asked if Joe had purchased the tickets for the trip to San Diego. She said yes, thinking he was talking about her tickets, and that was the end of the conversation. Perhaps he did not know Joe was just married otherwise he would have said congratulations Boo thought.

She asked Joe about the tickets when he returned and he told her he had. Why did she ask?

She told him a man had called and asked if he had the tickets purchased. She told Joe she had said "yes" but wasn't certain.

Joe began to get angry and becoming red faced told her to get her stuff together so they could get to the airport.

She thought that was an odd tone, but he was tired. She was tired too but tried to be understanding in the conversation. In hindsight, that episode was the beginning of the end of their marriage.

They managed to stay relatively happy for two more years before their nerves were beginning to fray and tempers began to flare. She was working part time in a spa mostly for the perks, doing facials and peels. There were some talented make-up artists on site and they loved to work on Boo because of her unique skin. That issue became important after a few more years went by.

Then, one day about three years prior to our meeting, Boo came home and found her husband in a real snit. She told him that maybe he needed another woman in his life. She said she obviously didn't complete him. In response he hauled off and knocked her across the room.

That was the first time she really needed the make-up artist. She had quite a shiner.

Those physical fights continued more frequently and he never talked about his work or why he would come home occasionally with black eyes or cuts and bruises. She was beyond caring.

That went on for the next three years, until right now. Last week was the last big blow up. Really the last! It was the fifth time she was at the shelter for any length of time. She never knew if Joe looked for her when she went away after a fight but just in case she always went to the shelter.

"When I came home the weekend of our last fight there was a phone message from a crying girl. The girl on the phone recording asked Joe if he knew how she was going to get her money back. I relayed the message to him and he just came apart. He threw me against the wall and hurled some of my china at me while I was on the floor. He was rushing forward to kick me so I grabbed his ankle and turned it quick so that he fell on the coffee table. He moaned and I ran out of the house."

"I called my brother to tell him what I had done and he said he would take care of it. Then I went to the women's shelter and that was the end of that," she sighed. Boo had exhausted herself telling us that. Then she smiled her beautiful big smile and chimed, "Good-bye and good-riddens."

Chapter Four

The big white van passed us on the right as we practiced correct yodeling technique and we turned our heads the other way, pretending not to notice them. After several attempts we realized that if we just repeated "old lady who" real fast we were producing a pretty respectable yodel.

We'd been on the road for over an hour and we were all talking at once most of the time. This was fun. This is what men and women conversations lack; the constant chatter, revealing intimate secrets, the nonsense and the understanding that just talking about anything is better than silence. Men are actually not that interesting. They do not know how to communicate funny and unforgettable anecdotes. They can cheat at cards or wish for a better golf game, but they cannot make small talk. Women, however can try on a funny bra and laugh about it for months, especially if the lighting is not flattering and the clerk enters the fitting room innocently showing a shocked expression. Women can date someone and remember what a bungling fool he was twenty years later, recalling his name and what he was wearing. We are fascinating and unbelievable creatures.

Boo was getting ready to change lanes so we could pull over and switch drivers when our car fell in behind that ominous white van again just south of Victorville. We were talking about the outlet shops coming up in the next few miles and decided not to spend more than two hours there regardless of how many stores we had not entered. That's when an incident with the white van created some unexpected heart palpitations.

The van slowed ahead of us. One of the two back doors of the van opened and an squatty, dirty appearing man stood there peeing on the road in front of our car, which splattered on our windshield, and then he threw a bundle, wrapped in a gray blanket, from the van. It bounced into the roadside ditch clogged with sagebrush and assorted litter.

I froze and my heart was literally pounding out of my sweater. I covered my mouth to keep from screaming, and I was shaking at the possibilities of what was in that blanket.

Boo hit the brakes and quickly pulled over as the van sped away.

All the car doors flew open and we jumped out of the vehicle and ran to the blanket. I heard the soft cry of a dog and almost fainted as the hurt rushed through me. We were all crying by the time we bent down to pull the blanket back.

It was a Doberman, maybe two years old, black and tan, with a large cut on a front leg. There was no collar. The dog was breathing heavily and looked at us in a way that said "I really need your help right now."

I was close to hysterical. Mattie, Lucy and Boo were all talking at once. I fired off a silent prayer to punish those guys before too long, hopefully in a very gruesome way. This is why we were on the road. This is why God wanted us to leave at the time we did and why the four of us were together. I could not believe what those bastards had done. I could only look and pet and cajole this beautiful animal. We each took one corner of the blanket moving her into the SUV where we could give her the love and protection she so deserved. She seemed very affectionate and tried to lick our hands. We adjusted her blanket in the area behind the back seat, putting the trash bag full of gowns under her head.

"I'll stay in the back with her," I said, cradling her head in my lap.

As vacations go this was not turning out that great and our carefully laid plans were definitely taking a new direction.

We had time to imagine the most obscene and painful things we would do to those cretins if we ran into them again. I wasn't sure how I would get the crochet hook into any one of their penises or squirt the perfume in their eyes, but it helped me over my anger to think that is what I would do.

All crying, we stopped at a convenience store for some soft dog food and bandages. Our newly rescued dog looked malnourished and dangerously thin. She was probably ravenous although obviously very frightened. Lucy got some ice cubes from a soft drink machine and rubbed them on the dog's lips hoping they would melt into her mouth. She seemed at peace with us. Her heart had stopped pounding wildly and almost felt regular. I could have sworn she actually was smiling.

We hadn't driven for thirty minutes when we spotted the bastards' white van parked in front of a 50's style diner that doubled as a funky Elvis museum at the Yermo junction. A stand alone restaurant it would be easy to park and get in and out.

People who love animals often have little control over their primal emotions when directly faced with animal abuse and I quickly convinced myself that any compassionate court in the land would hold us harmless for any vigilante justice that might befall these obscene men.

"Shall we take a gun inside?" Lucy asked as we pulled into the parking lot between the van and the gas station.

"I have mace," said Boo. "It's not acid, but it will stop their driving for a while. I think they will be very sorry for their disgustingly bad behavior today."

"I will go in with Boo," I said. "The memory of that hurt dog facing me on the highway makes me sick enough to do something really weird. I do have a crochet hook don't forget!"

Mattie and Lucy left the SUV to inflict some damage to the van's tires and hopefully slow any pursuit of us after what we expected to be an unpleasant encounter in the diner.

A Chevron station attendant adjacent to the van provided Mattie and Lucy with a small pointed punch and hammer necessary for their work. The attendant even offered his assistance when they told him what had happened. He went with them to the rear of the van and the three punched the back two tires in several places. Fortunately it was not dual axle. We hoped our flat tire attack would prevent them from following us for several hours.

Both Lucy and Mattie said they felt the vibrations of conversation, not so much hearing the words, but an eerie sound from within the van. They thanked the Chevron attendant and wondered if it was the anticipation of the coming situation or if they actually had heard someone inside. They wondered if perhaps only one of the men went in the diner to pick up meals and the others were inside the van box talking.

Mattie and Lucy came into the restaurant and reported the success of their tire flattening foray. Boo and I captured the booth behind the three large dark haired men whose order had just arrived at their table.

As quick as a cat Boo was at their table staring at them as if casting a spell. She picked up a steak knife that was on one of the sizzling steak plates and held it precariously close to the fat man on the end seat closest to us. His ears were like little pita bread hanging on a large round face. How do one's ears get so large I wondered? The two others that sat with him were dressed alike in filthy red plaid shirts and greasy black hair. They ate well, and frequently, judging from the size of their bloated stomachs pushing against the table in the booth.

"You bitches again? This might be our lucky day," said the scruffy one who had run us down in the coffee shop earlier that morning.

"Stay put," Boo said. As the fat one started to move toward her she punched the steak knife down into the table through the web between his fourth and fifth fingers causing him to cry out in surprise. Then he shut up immediately, willing to stifle the searing pain so no one would notice them. His face was beet red and oily sweat dripped off his chin and onto the table.

I spoke slowly to all three. "You are a pathetic blight on society. No doubt that feeling is shared by all who know you. We picked up the dog you threw out of the van and will keep her as evidence so the police can know what bastards you are. And peeing out of the back of the van, from that thumb sized link sausage, no doubt will be an offense of some measure, some small measure, if only a crime against nature."

The waitress was returning to the table so we needed to wrap up this little drama. Lucy intercepted the waitress and requested pie for the three at the table.

"I doubt if we will see you again this trip. The police should come for you shortly, but just know we are always ready for you. A bullet will certainly stop you degenerates before you have any chance to hurt us," I said.

Mattie, from the booth behind, had called the police and told them where the men were and the incidents that had taken place earlier. We could only hope they were close.

Boo shot pepper spray at the two other men before we turned to go. We heard their coyote-like yips as we exited the restaurant, quickly jumping into the SUV and heading west as fast as we could. We noticed flashing police car lights coming from the east and felt confident the three degenerate amigos would not be bothering us again.

"How is our baby doing back there?" Boo inquired of Lucy. We looked at the sorrowful Doberman lying under the soft blanket we brought for ourselves breathing regularly.

"Why not call her Baby? She will always be our baby," I said.

"I think we should put a little salve or balm on this open wound. It would heal better and keep the infection out." We'd forgotten to pick up some antibiotic salve when we bought the bandages, an unfortunate omission we now noticed. Who has something in their purse?" I asked.

"I have KY jelly in individually wrapped packages!" shouted Mattie. This comment should have prompted a number of intriguing questions but no one ventured to ask. After all, this was supposed to be a girl vacation. She rummaged through her bag throwing the contents every which way in search of the KY.

Handing it to me, I took the KY out of the wrapper and tried to release the plunger. I pushed it gently into the open end of the applicator but nothing happened. I put my face down to see if anything was in the tube and pushed the plunger a little more, and splat into my face went the KY. Looking straight at me, the girls waited a full three seconds before laughing. Then we all howled in unison, savoring the silliness of the moment and gooey mess on my face.

Eventually we got the KY on Baby and she licked my fingers as it glided across the wound. How we all loved this dog and hated those bastards at the restaurant. By now, we hoped, they were in jail making someone else miserable.

Mattie left our name when reporting the incident just in case they had questions or needed us to identify those bastards when we returned. We had some water in the little car cooler and a small dish with nuts, so we emptied the nuts and put water for Baby in the bowl. She drank sideways until the bowl was empty. We could not do enough for her. Thank you God, so much, I thought to myself.

We felt pretty confident for our safety now that those men were presumably in custody and so we stopped at a little restaurant in Primm Valley for a sandwich. We did not want to deal with the hassles of eating in Las Vegas. Our trip, now with a dog, might look a little different than our trip without Baby.

When we got to Las Vegas we would check into the hotel where our room had been reserved weeks ago and explain our situation with Baby. If they would not accept us with a dog perhaps they would at least give us back our money.

It is always so windy in the desert I thought. How did people stand this? My eyes were full of sand and my hair seemed full of dirt by the time we walked across the parking lot to the Yosemite Sam Casino diner. We could hardly wait for a bath in Las Vegas.

"Why don't I call the hotel from here and ask if we can have a dog in our room? If not, we should just stay here the first night," Lucy said.

That sounded like a great plan to the rest of us. It was already past two o'clock, and there were outlet stores, gambling, and nightly entertainment in Primm so a one night stay might actually be fun.

I phoned the hotel and they were appalled that we would even consider bringing an animal into their overpriced Strip hotel. They were, however, very generous and agreed to credit back our cards with the night's deposit and forward our courtesy chips to the hotel of our choice. We had purchased those with a dinner/show package, so they were not actually gratis. We could still be in Vegas for our show tomorrow night; just now we could relax and have some low maintenance fun.

We checked in at Primm explaining our situation with Baby and were assigned a two bedroom suite reserved for smokers because of possible dog odor from Baby.

Baby was still asleep when we went to the SUV to get her and the luggage. We gently lifted her out and set her on the ground to see if she could walk on her own. She laid there for a minute then cautiously got up and took very small steps staying close to us and going the distance to the room. I took the bedspread off one bed and made a nice place for her to lie in front of the window. We would go have a bite and bring back her dinner from the restaurant. She had water and she should sleep for at least another hour.

Upon entering the restaurant Mattie's phone rang and the calling party happened to be the police from Victorville, who were actually the responding police from the earlier restaurant call in Yermo.

"Is this the Mattie who called Victorville police regarding three men who threw a dog from the van?

"It is," she said. "How can I help you?"

"My name is Detective Ricky Khat. We need a better description of the men you earlier reported. Perhaps you could give those to our artist? Would that be possible?" asked the detective.

"Were they not at the café? I saw your lights coming as we were leaving the property. We had flattened two tires. They could not have driven away," Mattie said uneasily.

"We apprehended two of the men, their eyes were still watering, but the third got away. Judging from the contents in the van there was one perhaps even two others in the cab. They bolted when they heard the sirens. They were transporting nineteen illegals to Las Vegas. Two of the illegals in the van were dead, probably from suffocation. There was very little air or water in the back of that crowded space," he said. "These men are extremely dangerous and have been transporting illegals for many years right under our noses. One, whose hand had been pinned to the table with a steak knife, was gone. We have some nice skin samples for DNA. Good job I might add. One blinded by the spray in his eyes had some unflattering remarks to say about you. I find it hard to believe you look like they described, but we will see."

"Oh, my God, so do you have an idea of where these other two or three might be?" Mattie questioned.

"Not a clue. So if you don't mind I would like to bring an artist with computer to you or you to us and we can get some sketches out on the wire. Not a lot of people know the faces of these men," he said.

"Great and they know our faces all too well," Mattie replied.

"Perhaps you could tell us where you are staying and the three of us could drive to you in whatever amount of time it takes. We could have this wrapped up in a couple of hours, I am certain," said Detective Khat.

Mattie gave them our hotel in Primm Valley feeling that this would be easier and we would not have to back track.

"Good, we'll see you later this evening and just to be safe, don't answer your door unless I say "Merry Christmas," he said, a little laugh in his voice. With me will be Detective Juan Cortez and Detective Phillip Johns. We look nothing like the men who escaped, we are assuming."

"That's good news," Mattie said, and closed the phone.

"Well, you heard that I'm sure. There are either two or three men fleeing from the police, currently whereabouts unknown, who would probably have no problem killing us. Vague perhaps, but that's what I know right now. The police are coming from Victorville this evening to get more information and put together some facial features on the computer. Don't open the door unless they say Merry Christmas. Is this the best vacation you have ever been on Boo? Tell me you're not sorry you came with us?" Mattie asked.

Boo laughed and said, "Next to the day you asked me to come with you, this is the best time ever."

In the restaurant we played with our salads, looking over each others shoulders and keeping the knives in sight. Now we were making small talk to keep from getting scared.

We left the restaurant, not finishing our meal, with a couple of hamburger patties to go for Baby. I noticed at the same time as Boo, Mattie and Lucy how short our SUV appeared.

"The trailer is gone!" We shouted simultaneously.

Thank God our clothes were in the room. "Boo, we are so sorry. That was yours and Joe's and all of your china was in the trailer," I said apologetically.

Boo's face was no longer a beautiful tan but was quite white. We thought she may be in shock but she eventually looked at us and said, "Now is as good a time as any I guess to tell you a bit about my cargo. I would feel terribly sad if I did in fact lose my good china, but I lost Joe in that trailer!"

"Is that a wish? I asked, a little too happily.

"No," Boo said.

"Maybe I didn't hear that correctly, but did you mean a cup of Joe, an espresso Joe machine or a person called Joe?" I questioned in a little whisper.

Mattie and Lucy were staring, not in an accusatory way, but wanting to understand what she had just confided to us.

"Yes, Joe was in there. My brother clued me in when I came home from the shelter, but I thought since I would be taking the trailer with us I would just leave him somewhere in Las Vegas. His death was totally his own fault. He fell on the corner of the glass coffee table, which put a huge hole in his head. My brother said Joe was long beyond any help when he got to the house. Joe was already stone cold dead. You girls are not involved and I don't want to get you involved in my problems. I'll rent a car to go back to San Diego if you want to continue on with the SUV. Obviously the incriminating evidence is not in our possession any longer".

I personally felt no remorse for Joe or any anger towards Boo. I looked at Mattie and Lucy and they were looking at Boo with the same empty emotionless look I had. No one seemed sad.

"Let's all keep on going. This is not going to ruin our vacation. The more I heard about Joe the less I liked him anyway. Some people are just not meant to be in our life forever." Lucy and Mattie nodded and we turned towards our room as if nothing other than the theft had occurred.

"It looks like the license plates are on the roof of the car. They must not want us to phone in the number for identification," Boo noticed.

"You don't think it was "the men" do you?" Lucy asked.

"No, no, probably someone who needed more space or thought that the trailer had a six foot chest full of tools. They will be unpleasantly surprised when that box is opened. The bozos from Yermo couldn't have known we would stop here and they certainly could not be this far on foot. We were hauling ass since the diner," I said, still rather dumbfounded by the situation and my lack of emotion for what had happened to Joe. I checked my pulse.

"Let's go to our room and clean up, take a nap, go play slots, something. This is a very weird day," Lucy said.

Baby was waiting at the door needing a little potty break, so I took off my belt and gently guided her to the back of the hotel. She was getting her strength back and after her bath tonight she would be a new dog. She would definitely be the recipient of much attention from the four of us and, in spite or her recent ordeal, she apparently had hit the doggy lottery.

Lucy had showered and was combing out her hair. Boo was in the second bath showering and so Mattie and I amused ourselves surfing through the television channels while waiting our turn. I hated showers and was looking forward to a long bath.

We came to a local news channel just as the *Breaking News* was flashing across the screen.

"A young couple and child, burned inside their travel trailer, have been found by the police just outside of Victorville. A crowbar placed into the door handle and frame prevented the family from escaping the flames. Their identification has not been confirmed at this time. The police are questioning people in the trailer park to get any ID on the vehicle used to pull this trailer."

"Oh shit!" Mattie said looking at me.

Swallowing hard we ran to the others practically breaking down the door where Boo was bathing. Together we blurted out the tragic story from the news channel.

"Let's remain sane here. We have three guns and police on their way. Aim at the groin and throat and head. They might actually be smart enough to have on the bullet proof vests!" Boo said rather calmly.

I got out hair spray, curling irons, electric rollers, the coffee carafe; everything I could hurt myself with was a potential weapon. Wigs were placed on bed pillows as a diversion in case they broke in later. The pillows were placed on the queen beds in the first room adjacent to the front door. It seemed that would be the logical direction to look when entering the room.

It was five o'clock. We thought about writing poetry instead of gambling, counting our blessings instead of our winnings, just for tonight of course. We would feel better tomorrow when these men were in custody. Mattie and I jumped into and out of the showers so we could get the desert off of us before the police arrived. We toweled off, blew out our hair and threw ourselves into jeans and sweaters. Just as we sat to watch more television there was knock on the door. Baby gave a low growl and a little bark. I was ecstatic. She was fully alert and ready to protect us. We were holding onto each other and Mattie cried out, "Who is it?"

"Merry Christmas," a masculine voice from the other side of the door answered back.

I looked through the peep hole and thought I saw Cowboy. Was I dreaming? I felt flushed and wanted to jump him when he entered, but thinking he may turn and run I just told the others the one I could see did not look dangerous.

"Shall we open it?" Mattie asked.

"I've got the hair spray for the eyes just in case," Lucy said.

As we opened the door we saw some rather handsome men looking in at us. I almost didn't care if they had evil intentions. None of them looked even remotely similar to the men that we had encountered earlier that day.

"Hi, I'm Ricky, said my Cowboy look alike, this is Juan and the good looking guy on the end is Phillip. Juan is our artist and Phillip and I are at your service to protect and serve until this situation is under control." Ricky had a deep sexy voice.

Gads, I hope they don't get hurt! If we all lived through this, the possibilities were endless! I looked at the others. There was no more fear on those faces. Perhaps our dear friend with the KY was unhappy about using it on Baby, and I was sad I couldn't tell Ricky about last weeks dream.

"Come in please," Mattie said. "We have a kitchen table with four chairs over here or a sofa which may or may not be more comfortable. We have water and tea bags, some instant coffee and this package, which could be crackers or coffee filters! We haven't brought our cooler in from the truck yet where we have cashews and chocolate."

Phillip jumped up and offered to get the cooler from the SUV if one of us would show him the way.

Mattie was all over that. She did look damn nice with him. Both were blond and tan and could have been brother and sister if you did not know otherwise. She turned her head and gave us that "Thank you God" look, then turned back to Phillip and headed toward the door.

Boo tossed her the room key and the SUV key and asked that they take Baby, just in case she needed a little lawn break. We watched Baby get up from the bed we had made for her and start to stretch. Remembering then that she had some sore areas she walked out the door with a slight limp.

"Is that the dog they threw out of the van?" asked Ricky. "What a beautiful Doberman. If for no other reason I'd like to put the bastard out of his misery so it doesn't happen twice."

"It broke our hearts when we saw that happen, but she is coming along nicely and I think in a couple of days she will be able to run again," I said with a little crackle in my voice.

"That was one mean son of a bitch we found at the restaurant," Ricky said. "His eyes were still full of pepper spray. It took three officers to hold him for cuffs. He tried biting one, but luckily he missed. He looked like a rabies carrier," Ricky laughed.

"This probably is not what you had in mind for a vacation. Those aliens in the van will be sent back to Mexico, but they are still alive thanks to you. Another hour in that van and all would have been dead. Exhaust fumes were heavy in that box. They are being questioned now, but we don't expect to get much information from them. They are afraid for themselves and their families. They don't speak English and they have spent their life's savings coming to the United States. Now they'll be sent back with less than what they had before, in fact, far worse off," Juan said as he got his computer set up on the table.

"One of the men found dead in the van was only about sixteen. The other dead one could have been his father. They were side by side in the van and their shirts were the same fabric, hand stitched, probably by the same woman," Ricky said.

"Do you find this often," asked Lucy, "truckloads of aliens, starving or dying of thirst?"

"There are many found and caught coming across in various manners of transport, but usually they are in better shape. A lot of the young women that the coyotes don't want to be damaged are handled with care. They bring them for prostitution so they need to be careful."

"And the men need to be able to work right away so being dehydrated is not good. People who do this put no value on human or animal life. They are uneducated and morally bankrupt opportunists who prey on their victims' hopes and desperation. It pays well and they are not qualified for any other type of work. This is their best chance of getting any money. To me, they have much less value than those they are ridiculing and bringing across. They are scum, real bottom feeders," Ricky stated.

Boo asked if they knew the type of car or truck the men were driving now. She told them about the little trailer that had been stolen from the SUV, not bothering to mention traveling Joe's role in that tale of larceny.

"They are taunting us I think."

"The burned travel trailer with the bodies needed a good size vehicle as a pull. So they do have a hitch and a gas guzzling vehicle. Perhaps they are still trying to transport some people into Las Vegas. How large was your trailer?" Juan asked.

Boo said the trailer was about six feet wide and eight feet long. The trailer had a special tool box that was the width of the trailer and a lock down top.

"The tool box was full of personal items. I was moving from my home keeping memories of my past," she said.

"I am sorry to hear that," said Ricky. "I left everything when I moved. I guess I didn't have a trailer," he laughed, realizing that was not a very considerate remark.

"It's ok," Boo said. "It's probably better the trailer has disappeared. Sometimes you just need to get rid of past memories and it usually takes someone else to convince you. You might have kept things you no longer needed as well."

We nodded sympathetically towards Boo. I realized she was making a sly inside joke to the rest of us about Joe's body in the trailer. The fact that her comment seemed humorous gave me cause to worry about myself.

"I really know very little about the four of you other than Mattie called from the restaurant and Boo had a trailer," Ricky said as he looked at the hotel door. He shared a brief work history of the three of them, probably to put us at ease.

Ricky had been on the force for twenty years. I thought, to myself, that he was about six feet tall. Originally from Oklahoma, he moved to California's land of milk and honey in Riverside just three years ago. I suspected he might have a Cherokee heritage as his cheekbones were very predominant and his lack of facial hair was evident.

Phillip was a seventeen year veteran and at least six foot three inches tall with huge hands and masses of blond hair. I wondered about his other extremities, but, being a lady, kept my thoughts to myself. He had been born and lived his entire life in Ontario, California.

Juan had been a detective and sketch artist for only six years. He had previously owned and managed a gym where he also worked as a personal trainer. He still owned the gym but seldom visited it anymore as police work occupied most of his waking hours. Juan's extra special talent was his uncanny ability to visualize and sketch anyone from just a hint of a description. Of course to myself I thought he looked like Desi Arnez and a perfect match for Lucy.

We all went to the kitchen where Lucy, I, Ricky and Juan sat at the table. Boo was leaning up against the counter watching the door, waiting for Mattie and Phillip and Baby to get back. They were taking a lot of time to go to the SUV, but maybe they were getting to know one another or waiting for Baby to do her poop bag thing.

Juan was putting facial features together from Lucy's description of the men she saw. He was very good at his profession and we were amazed at the similarity of the finished computerized portraits.

It was almost seven o'clock and we were getting a little hungry. As soon as Mattie got back we would go to a café in the hotel casino.

There was a knock at the door and Ricky jumped up to answer. It was Mattie and Baby.

"Where is Phillip?" Ricky questioned.

"He said he wanted to walk the casino parking area and see if he saw our trailer or anyone who had mismatched Arizona plates. Phillip said the people who were killed earlier were from Arizona. He wanted to phone your office to see if any of the men had been apprehended and should be back here shortly."

We were all wearing jeans and sweaters, a far cry from the glamorous clothes we had anticipated wearing this week. And yet, a slight change of pace might be relaxing and help lift our spirits.

"Would it be fitting for us to have our first date at dinner tonight?" Ricky inquired with some levity in his voice.

"That would be wonderful," I said. "We had to abandon our lunch a little early after speaking with you about the non-capture of the men at the restaurant." I was smiling.

We told Ricky and Juan we would put on some lipstick, fluff our hair and be ready to have some dinner in thirty minutes. Ricky and

Juan were going to their room down the hall while we rearranged ourselves. We would meet them in the hall outside their room.

We were feeling much less vulnerable with these lawmen in tow.

I'd actually been feeling pretty secure with Boo around knowing she could handle situations that I might have had a problem managing, but the men added a whole new level to my comfort. And as an unexpected bonus they were very easy to look at and all differently interesting.

When we left the hotel room at seven forty-five Phillip was back and talking to Ricky and Juan in a hushed tone in the hall.

"Is everything ok?" I asked.

"I'm concerned that there are a lot of people in the parking area and in the casino. Maybe we should stay out of sight and just call out for some food. I moved your car directly behind this building in a three sided stall so there is not an immediate view of the vehicle. I changed the license plate also, so if someone is looking for your SUV they will assume it is someone else's and drive on. There is a set of the keys on the front tire, driver's side."

"I think if we keep together," Boo said, "we should be alright, right? I'd really like to stretch my legs a bit and I don't like feeling like a prisoner locked in the room here."

"We'll stay together," Ricky cut in, and off we went to get a bite at the closest café in the casino.

It was crowded, Phillip was right. We shoved our way to the line at the café and looked at faces surrounding us as we waited for our seven person seating call. The smell of cigarettes always was annoying, but we could hang our clothes tonight to air out before packing tomorrow.

"Ricky Khat, party of seven, please follow me." We were shown to a table in the center of the room, which Ricky immediately declined and pointed to the corner table which was in need of cleaning. "If you don't mind the wait for cleaning," the hostess said, in an annoyed voice, "you can have that area." We went to stand by our chosen table looking to see who might be watching. There seemed to be little interest in us which made us feel a little better and so we loosened up and started smiling a bit more. We arranged the seating, boy, girl, boy, girl until we ran out of genders.

The beverage waiter came to the table. He looked suspicious to me but after the day's earlier events, everyone did. We ordered individual glasses of wine because we each wanted a different type.

There was very little we knew about each other so we took turns introducing ourselves properly by giving short personal histories sprinkled with sometimes revealing, sometimes amusing anecdotes.

We learned more about Boo as she was telling of her childhood in St. Croix. Her father was a pro boxer so Boo knew a great deal about boxing and physical fitness. She was approximately six feet tall, but always referred to her height as five feet twelve inches. It made Joe happier that Boo sounded not so tall.

"My longest relationship has been Joe and boy do I wish I had only known him for a short time. He had an export business that I knew very little about. When he went to work he would not always come home at night and that led to a lot of harsh words and suspicious tension between us."

"Is he still your husband?" asked Ricky.

"Yes, he is still my husband. He is traveling tonight and I honestly have no idea where he is going to end up. He'll be surprising someone with his presence tonight I'm sure."

"Was he in favor of your coming on this trip?" asked Phillip.

"Oh, no, he has no idea of what is happening this week. He is in the dark," Boo sighed.

"We are all so blessed to have Boo with us on this trip," I said quickly. "It was just a fluke we met. I think we all feel like life long friends, secure knowing we will share secrets and remain best of friends till death due us part!"

The waiter was back and we ordered and lied about having to be at a show so they would hurry the order. I noticed the waiter had a tattoo on his right hand of what looked like a hawk. It was kind of interesting but the veins in his hand seemed to cut thru it at odd angles so that when he moved his fingers to pick up the glasses it looked like the hawk was either going to fly or throw up.

My personal tattoos were eyebrows and eye liner. Perhaps less effective than a screaming eagle, but they served their purpose well.

Mattie was talking about her divorce and how she and her ex were still really good friends, just not sleeping together friends. He was remarried, but before he did marry his current wife he asked Mattie if she would remarry him. She told him "no thanks" and wished him well. Mattie had been divorced for 10 years and there seemed no need for a man in her life at this point. She had a class of pre teen dancers now that were the light of her life. They were from privileged families and it allowed Mattie the time and money she wanted to do volunteer work with the humane society.

Mattie was a fabulous volley ball player and on my best exercise day she could go twice the time. She looked twenty-five, not forty-one. She had zero body fat and no tolerance for people who ate poorly and got fat. We always insisted that Mattie order lunch first. She kept Lucy and me in shape by always allowing us the courtesy of explaining why our selection should not be ordered.

Ricky talked about his first wife, who was actually his only wife, and how that relationship had lasted only two years. She was too young and too materialistic, attributes which he finally realized after almost two years into the marriage. They divorced in a semi-friendly manner and she moved from California to the East coast which delighted him immensely. I wanted him to keep talking. His voice was deep and covered you like a fluffy blanket when he spoke directly at you. He knew it and the waitress loved it too. She would talk directly to him when asking about anything at our table. She was young and looking for some return admiration. We all saw it, recognized it and remembered what that need was like.

"Shall we take dessert back to the room or have it here?" Lucy asked.

Where did she put dessert? Lucy was slender which showed off her new C-cups. Her auburn red hair was just shoulder length and she wore her makeup like the art she loved, perfect in every way. It was like a clear varnish had been put over her face. She still shaped her lips a little like Lucille Ball, but maybe I was the only one that noticed.

"Let's have it here," said Phillip. "We should stay together as long as possible."

I wanted to know more about Phillip. He was being very quiet and seemed more withdrawn than Ricky or Juan.

The dessert tray rolled by and we all selected something different so we could spoon off of each other's plate. In just a short time we were becoming very much like old friends, the seven of us.

Over dessert Phillip said he was an only child, very much favored by an aunt with whom he spent most of his teen years accompanying on fabulous trips. She loved to bum around Europe, but not alone. The aunt was a beautiful blond woman and Phillip was a handsome teenager and she loved being with him in public. His parents were not interested in traveling and did not object to his being with his aunt. He was in England with her, ready to visit Buckingham Palace, when she was hit by a motorist who was drunk. Phillip ran to her and when the man finally got out of his car to see what had happened Phillip beat the shit out of him. His beautiful aunt died that afternoon and he felt utterly lost and despondent when he finally returned home.

"I was so angry because he was drunk and did not feel the pain of my striking him. I only wanted to kill drunken people for months after that. It was a year before I decided to redirect my anger and disappointment into police work. If I could make a difference and keep someone from the type of death my aunt went through that would make my decision worth something," Phillip said.

Phillip had never been married. He was about forty-five I figured with beautiful blond hair and tan like Mattie. I think Mattie reminded Phillip of his aunt. We finished our desserts and were almost too full to move.

"Anyone want to play the slots?" I asked.

"Let's do that tomorrow after a good night's sleep and after the crowds thin out somewhat," said Ricky. "We're spending the night because it's the weekend and I don't think you are safe enough to be alone."

Ricky left cash for the bill on the table, waved to our waitress and we were off to our rooms. I noticed that the beverage waiter was talking to a deranged looking character by the cashier's cage. He saw me too, but did not acknowledge me.

We all went into our room for a final check of closets and areas of concern. Ricky checked the window to be certain we could get out, but also to be certain the security pole against the door would stop any unwanted entry into the room.

Baby was peacefully asleep on her bed. She was definitely on the mend. I hoped I would be the one that could keep her. We all wanted to own her and we all had room for her, but we could talk about that when we got home to San Diego. After all, Lucy had a cat already.

"Let's take Baby to our room so we can take her out if she needs to go. We'll take the blanket and guard her with our lives. If you have to leave in a hurry she won't be able to travel as fast as you. I promise she will be safe." I trusted him so we gave Baby kisses before she went with the three of them.

"You are just down the hall my sweet." She licked my hand and I almost cried. "She understands," I assured Boo, Lucy and Mattie.

Ricky gave us a key to their room two doors down the hall. All of us were on the ground floor which was our choice. There were large windows to the outside.

We all had cell phones and it was time to put everyone's number into memory.

I looked at my watch and it was almost eleven. I was tired and looking forward to a long bath before bed, not just the quick shower I had earlier. I loved soaking. The evening, although fun, was exhausting and certainly not as planned for our first big night out.

Ricky, Phillip and Juan left and headed down the hall. We were almost too tired to talk, but managed to comment on how darling the policemen were.

I was fond of Ricky, Mattie had her eyes on Phillip and Lucy wasn't shy about wanting to touch Juan. Joe had been such an unrelenting disappointment that I thought Boo was probably not considering a new relationship at this time but it was fun having something else to think about besides the monsters we had encountered earlier. Who could set people on fire, especially a family with a child? I so hoped that poor family was not alive or at least asleep when that happened. These were very sick men.

We all showered or bathed again, put on tee shirts and headed for the back bedroom where we would sleep two to a bed. We made certain the wigs on the pillows in the front bedroom just barely showed from under the covers and left the door ajar, locking ours. I could only hope any intruders would go to the right first if they entered, giving us time to get out the window.

I looked at the clock at 1:15 and felt more comfortable about the night ahead. I was clean, no make-up, my hair was still damp, but I felt good in my t-shirt and the hotel sheets, hopefully free from bed bugs. I actually felt fabulous.

Chapter Five

It seemed like I'd only been asleep five minutes when the sound of gunshots from the hall startled me awake. We were all out of bed in less than twenty seconds, grabbing for our phones and racing for the large window. "My God!" I screamed, pulling the safety bar from the window frame.

We pushed out the screen, hearing it land on the blacktop outside and I wondered if Ricky and the guys were involved in the gunshots. Out of the window we jumped and headed for the parking lot. Passing the men's bedroom on the run we noticed it was dark inside and began to fear the worst. Then I thought of Baby and wanted to turn and go back.

"Keep going," Boo said, "they promised Baby would be safe. It is us they want to kill. We are the only ones able to identify them."

Crowding next to the SUV we waited for Boo to get the keys off the front tire and open the doors.

We jumped in, left the lights off, backed out of our space and raced through the back parking lot to the freeway sign just at the end of the lot. The freeway entrance was right there and we headed north to Las Vegas.

"Do you think we should have gone south to confuse them?" Mattie asked.

"There is nothing in that direction for quite some time," I said. "We can be in Las Vegas in a half hour. There is little traffic at this time of the morning. If we drive straight into the Freemont area where more people will be hanging around we will be harder to find."

It came to our attention, all at the approximate same time, that we had no clothes and only two phones, and only one with a range for this area.

Lucy shrieked, "Shit, what about our clothes, our money, and our purses? I grabbed my phone from under the pillow, but that's all."

"Are the guns in the glove compartment?" I asked.

"Yes, are you thinking maybe we can rob a clothing store?" Boo laughed, somewhat nervously.

We did not think to keep any clothes in the car. There was silence for a couple of minutes and then Boo said, "What's in the garbage bag in the back?"

"Oh good God," we laughed, "the trashy evening wear!"

"There are five dresses and three pairs of heels, one pair of tennis shoes, badly damaged, and one pair of flip flops. They are absolutely atrocious. We were embarrassed to take them into the women's shelter so we kept them in the back of the SUV until we could get rid of them in Las Vegas," Lucy said

"Lucky for us you did not give them away," said Boo. Let's try the guy's hotel room.

There was no answer so we tried the emergency number on the one phone which covered this area. It went to answering machine first then to a voice taking our information. Lucy was telling them to go to the hotel in Primm and the police there would know what to do. She could only hope that made sense.

I could not imagine wearing a single one of those dresses, but it was our only choice without money or identification.

We sped on past Spring Mountain, past Sahara Boulevard until we arrived at the exit that would take us to the Golden Nugget Hotel. It kept us in the middle of the activity where we needed to be.

"On the west side of the hotel there is a parking lot. Let's go to the third floor and we can don these dresses and see if we can find some help. Parking is free so we don't have to pay to park. There is very little lighting on the third floor, so let's go to a corner near the stairwell," I said.

We found a good spot, jumped out and grabbed the bag from the back. It was flat from Baby laying on it earlier and I could hardly imagine what those dresses were going to look like at this point.

Empting the garments on the hood of the SUV and spreading them out, side by side, verified everything we had told Boo about the dresses. We stood shaking our heads. The halogen lights in the garage gave them a special sickly pallor that was hard to describe.

"Holy Crap!" Lucy said.

Boo laughed, "I see why you might have been embarrassed to give these to anyone! Luckily we don't have to find a favorite color. They are all horrible."

"None of these are going to look good, so does anyone care what they get?" Lucy said.

"Just give me what is on top. Three are spandex, so there should be no fitting issues. That one on the end looks like a wrap dress, so it will work also. That blue one seems to be missing fabric from the thigh down. Do you think someone took out the inside slip part? I think that might have been Monica Lewinsky's dress."

"It looks too small for any of us so these first four are the ticket," Mattie cringed.

"That would be the ticket we receive from the fashion police?" Lucy laughed.

"Here goes, and without lingerie," I said. "There is not actually a back or a front on this dress. I guess it is either or!" I gasped.

Lucy was wiggling into her dress, which had slits to her waist. Her perfect new boobs were just the answer for the tight stretch across her chest. There were two missing buttons on the V in the back, but no one would notice.

"I like the longer arms on yours. I am jealous!" I laughed.

"Of course you are, Lucy said. You should have these slits to your ass! I am showing cotton undies! These are sleeping gauge underwear!"

Mattie was struggling into the yellow mesh mini. "My goodness God, this may become one of my favorite colors!" The entire dress looked like fishnet stockings in yellow, with a small amount of fabric on the breast and the crotch area. "Whew," she said when she finally got it located on the right parts of her body. "It's a lot of work to look this bad!"

We turned to look at Boo who ended with the wrap dress which was just enough fabric to wrap around her fabulous curves.

"Does this have a belt, I hope?" Boo asked. "There is one button at the waist here, but I don't have a lot of faith in it holding for very long."

"Here is the belt I walked Baby with. It's not a perfect match, but it adds certain panache," I said.

"I have never liked red. I always thought it was whorish. Was that a premonition? I think this scoop is the back. What do you think?" I said and I squeezed into what could have been a long tube top with a shoestring tie for the neck.

We stood back and looked at one another and began laughing. We laughed and laughed and laughed. We laughed until we had to go to the bathroom, and found it handy that we were in the corner parking stall. I so wanted my camera and then remembered the cell phone had a camera feature. I took the picture and then called the numbers we had for Ricky, Phillip and Juan. No one had answered for the last hour. Where were they? I prayed they were not dead, lying in the room without help, bleeding to death. What was Baby doing? Please God, keep her safe I thought.

"I am going to call 911 again to see what they discovered at the hotel. There must be a problem with the guys. They are still not answering," I said.

"Good idea," Boo said. "We had better get downstairs and see if we can find a place to hide or someone to help us out. Phone the Vegas police while you're dialing."

As I dialed, my phone went dead. Lucy tried the other phone and got through to the police in Victorville. "They will give me no information over the phone!" Lucy said.

Boo had flip flops on and I wore the four inch heels that were a size too small. Mattie and Lucy had hideous shoes on, but not a bad fit. I hoped our travels would not be long; I'd experienced small shoe blisters and they were so painful.

We still had our two cell phones, unfortunately no identification and were leaving the guns in the SUV. We headed down the stairs to street level and came out in front of a pawn shop.

Ducking into the pawn shop, knowing we were dressed like four prostitutes from the poorer side of town, we hoped the owner would take pity on us. We saw our reflections in the large mirror that greeted us as we entered.

"Is that us? We look like the original dirty girls!" Lucy screeched.

"Let's go back for the gun!" said Boo.

Mattie and I were holding our hands over our mouths. I did not know if we were going to laugh or getting ready to throw up.

"Christ, my hair," Lucy squealed. "What a nest!"

Our dresses were beyond "what not to wear", but throwing in the tragic hair and lack of make-up there was not a shred of glamour that might generate sympathy. No purse, no brush, no credit cards, just our good health! And when you've got your health, you've got blah, blah, blah.

Chapter Six

An Amazon parrot, perched on a hat rack in the corner of the pawn shop, screeched, "Customer."

"Quiet," said the owner.

"Quiet," echoed the parrot.

"May I help you?" asked a not so friendly voice from behind the display counter. Perhaps he was Chinese. He was short, smug and looking at us like we carried an incurable disease. His hand did not extend for ours nor did his eyes actually meet our eyes. His eyes were bouncing from body to body. I felt he was looking for something that might be appealing, but not finding anything remotely close.

"Well, our story," started Mattie, "began this morning when we were coming to Vegas for a little trip and"

Lucy interjected, "then we were terrorized by these men who, for some reason, wanted to harm us so we turned them into the police."

"Police," the parrot echoed.

And Mattie said, "then they followed us to a hotel and stole our trailer and"

"Trailer," said the parrot.

"Shut up," said the owner to the parrot.

"Shut up," said the parrot.

"We don't know if they stole it," said Boo, "but someone did and then last night they broke into our room and we had to leave without our clothes or our bags or anything."

"And the policemen, down the hall, did not respond," Lucy stated hurriedly.

"What policeman?" the pawn shop owner butted in.

"Policeman," repeated the parrot.

"We had policemen come to take the information on the men that wanted to harm us," I said, "but then we heard the guns last night."

"What guns?" said the shop owner.

"Guns," mocked the parrot.

"The guns we heard before we went out the window of our hotel," I said.

"Where were police?" He asked again.

"Police," said the parrot.

"We don't know. We don't know if they are alright because they did not answer their phone," cried Lucy.

We were all talking at once when he turned out the lights and told us to leave the shop.

"I no need trouble here," he said. "You leave shop now. You come back when you not look like whores. This area is protected by Danni and he no like other women working his corner."

"Whores," said the parrot. "Whores, whores, whores," the parrot kept repeating.

"We are not whores," I said. "We just want to find a place to hide from the men who are chasing us. They want us dead. Do you understand what we are saying? Perhaps you could loan us enough money for a hotel tonight and we will pay you tomorrow when the police come to find us and bring our purses."

"Here, ten dollar for phone. Give me phone. I no help you and you go now. This my home and I want family safe," he said as he pointed to the door. We took the money quickly.

He produced a gun from behind the counter and pointed it at Mattie because of her proximity to him.

"Out," he shouted. "Out, now!"

"Out now, out now, out now," the parrot repeated.

We edged our way out of the shop, all four of us going through the door at the same time. We went to the first major street, which was Fremont. It was very bright with the overhead canopy of lights shining on our poorly made up faces. The yellow tinge of the lights made us appear jaundiced, which, as hard as it is to believe, made us look worse than before.

"What now, Sissy? Did we draw life's short straw today? I think we need to steal a passerby's purse!" Lucy suggested with a furtive look, craning her neck in search of an easy grab.

"It will be fine. We have ten dollars!" I assured Lucy and looked to Boo for some emotional support.

"We'll be ok," said Boo. "We just need to find a place to stay the rest of this night while we keep trying to contact the boys. They must be on their way here by now. Maybe this is just one of those areas where there is poor reception."

"You girls should not be on this block," drawled a voice from behind us.

We turned to see a rather nice looking hooker with two friends leaning on the building. They had on low cut white tops, black skirts with mesh stockings and open toe sandals with ankle laces. Their faces were made up rather plainly for hookers, much nicer than those I had seen in movies.

"Danni is not going to like seeing new girls here. Especially when they are not his girls," said the auburn haired girl. "Are you here from Reno? Your clothes are not from Vegas shops. Were you brought in by the Mexicans? Danni really hates the Mexican importers," she said.

Another little red head standing in the back came forward and looked at Lucy eye to eye.

"Is that your own hair or are you wearing a wig?" She reached out to touch Lucy, but Lucy backed up not knowing what to expect.

"No, this is pretty much my own. It's colored of course, but my own," Lucy said sheepishly.

"It's very pretty," she said. "If we become working friends maybe you could tell me what color to buy? Maybe you could even do it for me. I would pay you."

"Sure," Lucy said, "maybe tonight we could get the color at a drug store and you could pay me then?"

"I'm working for another four hours, but if you are still around, come back to this corner and see if I got busy. Maybe I might still be here, who knows?" she giggled.

"Here comes Danni," one of the girls said in a low voice. "Gotta go for now, good luck!"

The three of them turned and strolled on down Freemont just as a long Cadillac limo pulled up to us on the street.

"Get in," came a man's voice from deep within the limo.

"We don't need you, thank you though," came Mattie's voice, sounding a little unsure and not knowing who she was talking to or why.

"That's not a question, just get in."

We looked at one another and rather than run, because none of could, except for Mattie, we filed into the limo and sat four abreast, very quietly, on the seat facing backwards across from the two men on the seat facing us.

"You ladies look horrible. Do you agree?" he asked.

"Yes," we said in unison.

"Are you trying for shabby chic?" He said with a little laughter in his voice.

"These clothes were donated and it's all we had in the car when we jumped out of our hotel window and drove to Las Vegas," Lucy said.

"This could be a very interesting story," said the deep voice.

"My name is Danni. Many of the girls in this town work with my family and I think I have a very nice selection of women for any man's taste. You four fit into an element of artistic appreciation that I have had very few requests for to date. I am not saying that this could not be a new profitable market for me. Some cowboy, just off the range, that has had little experience with women who have had their hair done, a bath, manicure, pedicure, and new clothes might just succumb to the fascination and charm, but let's not chance it shall we?. Let's get you looking like women who I would personally be proud of and see what happens from there." He nodded to the other man in the car.

"JR, take us to the Penthouse," Danni instructed the driver.

We were very quiet; not knowing what words might come out if we chose to speak.

These two men were actually very nice looking. Where is my brain? I should be afraid, even perspiring, certainly not admiring my captors. I would say they had some African American and some Caucasian heritage. There were no fur coats or layers of chains around the neck and no hat or tam or garish overcoat. Earrings were noticeably missing and I could see only one diamond on the other person's hand next to the one named Danni.

Both were dressed in dark suits with white shirts. I could almost see my reflection in their high polished shoes. Thank God it was blurred. I guessed they were very tall because their legs almost met ours from across the area between the seats. They had sheepish grins on their faces and judging from the limo, they had their finances under control.

We drove in silence for a few minutes and then we pulled through an extremely tall security gate which surrounded a ten or twelve story building. The limo pulled up to the front and a smiling bellman jumped to attention and had the doors open as the car came to a stop.

"Ladies, please, you first," said Danni. "Go thru the lobby to the elevator on the right."

We walked with whatever pride we had left, shoulders back, breasts out. I was certain my feet were bleeding, but I tried not to limp.

As Danni and his friend entered the elevator I suddenly felt very safe. He pushed the "P" and we were heading up. These were not the feelings I had expected fifteen minutes ago. No one uttered a word.

The highly polished brass elevator doors opened into the penthouse, revealing an exceptionally spacious room with gold and crystal glistening like a desert sunset. Just a few minutes earlier we were in Hell and now we were somewhere on the outskirts of Heaven. There were several women lounging in the large open living area. The fragrance of their perfumes collided in my nostrils. I was jealous they had a fragrance and I had a smell. Perhaps there were more people in other rooms that were out of sight, the ones that would come to kill us. A large somewhat older man sat at the bar talking on the phone.

The guests all turned and looked in disbelieving horror as we walked into the room. The mood instantly changed from merriment to dread. Not a word was spoken by anyone. Perhaps they had their tongues removed. Terror seemed to show in the girls facial expressions. Had they witnessed what happened to girls dressed like this before?

Danni turned to us, "I apologize for not introducing Josh, my brother, to you in the car. My manners were in short supply. An unexpected encounter with some very unsavory characters left us rather speechless and then seeing the four of you, well we were already speechless, where do you go from there?"

"The man at the bar is our father. We have a family business, a good business with an extended family that you may wish to become part of, should you stay." He nodded towards his father.

"Now, if you would follow Sylvia, (who just appeared from thin air) you will be taken to a room down the hall and given time to freshen up and put on some, shall we say, more appropriate clothes? You might notice that we try to keep our colors to black and white, or white and white, or black and black, you decide. There will be a choice for you so please feel free to mix and match as you see fit. We like a professional appearance, not the "off the bus look." He smiled at Sylvia with the most beautiful teeth I had ever seen.

Lucy, not knowingly, had dropped her phone in the limo and Danni had picked it up. He chose not to return it when we went down the hall with Sylvia.

We followed Sylvia down the hall as instructed. At this point I would have followed Son of Sam. We were tired, dirty, no doubt stinking and looking forward to any change of clothes.

Sylvia opened the door and we were in awe at the beauty of the room. A light pink moiré silk fabric covered the furnishings and a bolder version of crème and rose covered the walls. The drapes, which were definitely black-out weight, were crème with rose pulls. The floor was covered in soft pink plush carpet and just enough tinted mirrors to create warmth and if possible make us look better.

Beyond this room into the next space were several lovely shower stalls, I counted six, with gold fixtures and pastel tiles. There were blow dryers, rollers, make-up, shampoos and soaps all displayed neatly by each stall. Individual make-up chairs with mirrors were on the opposite wall.

"I could make this my permanent home in a heart beat," I said to everyone, trying not to sound too enthusiastic.

"Me too," said Boo touching the blown glass containers full of lotions.

Lucy and Mattie were still looking around and wincing at their images in the mirrors.

"We actually walked around a small area of this city looking like this," said Lucy. "People actually saw us. Let's pray no pictures were taken for local newspapers. I can never run for president now. Let's hope what happens in Las Vegas really does stay in Las Vegas!"

"You ladies may feel free to use whatever you wish. The closets are full of clothes, any of which you may choose to wear. I am certain you will find your sizes. Shoes are behind the mirrored doors at the end of the clothing. Be as comfortable as possible," Sylvia said in a kitten soft voice. "I know Danni and Josh are anxious to talk with you further. If you need me press the buzzer on the counter just over there and I will come in," said Sylvia.

Sylvia left us then and we looked at one another wondering what to do first. It was going to be a project in itself getting out of these clothes. I rang the bell mostly to see if she would come back but also to ask for scissors. She showed up immediately, laughing at my request.

"She is a beauty," I said. "Do you think she is like the house mother?"

"I don't believe she is as old as we are, but perhaps," Mattie said.

"Does anyone look as old as we do right now? Should I leave our only ten dollars for a tip?" I giggled.

"Start cutting me out of this thing," Mattie said. "I don't know how I got my arms in this mesh."

We laughed and cut and laughed some more with no thought of what the next few hours would present.

Chapter Seven

"Let me try the numbers," said Ricky. "They must be in serious trouble if not one of them can answer the phone. Oh Christ, I really let them down."

"Wait, someone is answering the phone," he said.

"Yes, may I help you?" a man's voice crooned on Lucy's phone.

"Where in the hell is Lucy and who in the hell are you? If you hurt those women you will die a long slow death you son of a bitch," Ricky spewed into the phone.

"Right now they are fine, thank you for asking. Once they are cleaned up they may be worth quite a bit. I will be turning this phone off now." Danni was smiling to him self and the line went dead.

Ricky went white. His head ached and he was still vomiting from the gas that had been used in the room earlier. All three had been out for over five hours. The ambulance arrived at the hotel shortly after the call from Lucy, but the paramedics could not bring them out of a dead sleep. The emergency crew found rubber tubing under the door that filled the room with a noxious gas as the police slept. Baby was in the bathroom on her blanket and got only half the dose that the police had inhaled. She was doing fine now as she lay in the back of the vehicle with the window opened full for fresh air. None of the detectives had experienced that type of toxic gassing before.

"Is this the new war we are fighting?" said Phillip, when they were being revived.

Juan started to comment and threw up again.

"So much for the bullet proof vests we wore," Ricky said, his blood drained white pallor and blue lips just starting to show a glimmer of his previous well toned face.

"Perhaps they have drugged the girls and that's why they did not answer their phones?" said Phillip.

"The voice that answered Lucy's phone was more refined than those bastards in the restaurant. It was definitely not Mexican. He could be their boss I suppose, but now what?" Ricky said puzzled by the turn of events.

"And why did he answer the phone?" asked Juan, finally able to hold his head straight.

Heading north on the strip there were millions of places the girls could be held. There were pickpockets, whores, winos, street vendors and gamblers all out crowding the streets. It was eight o'clock in the morning. What a world. Did those card pushers ever go home? Ricky remembered times when he would bring his wife to Las Vegas and she would talk to those guys as they handed her cards to the topless shows. She would actually seek them out, telling them they should appreciate women more. It was good that relationship had ended he thought, his brain still fuzzy.

"Let's stop at Circus Circus, just for a breakfast, then go to the local police and see if they can help us out a little."

They parked the car and got Baby out for a little stretch in the parking lot. With the anticipation of a long overdue breakfast they placed her back in the vehicle, leaving a window opened for fresh air. She was breathing very easily and her eyes were filled with a look best described as canine understanding. "I will kill the bastard that hurt you Baby," Ricky declared.

Finding a clean booth in the casino café with a window view of the parking lot the three sat and ordered breakfast while looking around for any faces that might appear as out of place or as agitated as they were feeling. They were all out of place as far as faces go.

Who looked like they belonged in this city? A good looking tourist could be an escapee or a priest for all they knew.

They felt dejected and frustrated as they sat in the café booth eating dollar ninety-eight steak and eggs. Their search for the girls seemed an impossible task.

"Save some steak for baby," Phillip reminded them. "Roll up a pancake too. No syrup." They found some diversion from their malaise in doting on the one responsibility they managed to handle correctly.

Phillip was facing the parking lot and saw an attractive young Mexican girl step from a car in front of the adjacent hotel entrance. She was probably not more than fifteen but she walked with an elegant gait and was dressed in a distinctly provocative mini-skirt. The girl did not enter the hotel but loitered casually about fifty feet away from the valet parking desk.

"Ricky, check out that senorita on the other side of the street. She was just dropped off and seems to be waiting there, perhaps to work the hotel. It's hard to tell if she has an appointment or is supposed to find her own."

"I think I will see if I can buy an hour. She looks more my type than yours!" Ricky laughed leaving the table.

"What's my type?" Phillip yelled after him.

Phillip and Juan watched as Ricky approached the smiling girl and began talking to her. She was a looker and she knew it.

She held her hand out, palm up.

Ricky escorted her back to the booth. Perhaps he told her it was a threesome and at this time in the morning they imagined that could be good money. Her manager would be happy with that.

"Well boys, before we get that room, I thought we could introduce ourselves and see what Paula has to offer," Ricky said.

She sat on Juan's side of the booth. She was petite with bright eyes and a closer look suggested she was probably Cuban, not Mexican. She was more cute than sophisticated but presented herself as a class act in the city more known for floosies.

"Do you speak English Paula?" Juan asked.

"Yes sir, I do. I lived in Brazil but was schooled in Central America. I take care of myself now and gradually pay back the family that paid for my education. My parents sent me to a private school when I was twelve and the school owners teach us everything we need to be successful and then we come to the United States and work. They gave my parents money for me to learn at their school," she said in a soft voice. "I pay back the family in Las Vegas that works with the school now that I am here. I pay on my own schedule which is nice for me so I can pursue more schooling."

This was all new. These girls were not stuffed in a compartment and brought across the border in a van or worse. These girls were bought from their parents and educated to work at their new Las Vegas homes in the States. It seemed like a rather unusual arrangement and she had Ricky's full attention.

How large of an operation could this possibly be Ricky wondered? Why had he not heard of this before? All of the attention was going to the unlucky ones that paid to get across the border and then had to work for years to continue paying over and over again. This was a much smoother and well organized business. Actually this was like going to school and paying back student loans. No one told the girls they had to be prostitutes when they came to the United States. They just had a stated monetary amount due to whoever had paid the school to educate them.

Ricky's head was still reeling from the fumes he had been exposed to earlier. They exchanged looks over Paula's head.

"Do you have someone picking you up here soon?" Ricky asked.

"No, no. I will call when we have had our time together," Paula said.

"Paula, we would like to buy an hour of your time and maybe just talk about you and your new family. We are new in town and don't know a lot about the city, like where the most action happens," Phillip said.

Paula gave them a little frown.

"Don't get us wrong," said Phillip, "we don't want another girl, and if we stay for a while, how would we get in touch with you again? Do you have a number or could we come to a location you might work from?"

"We work mostly in the Old Las Vegas area, but our family does not like us there alone, only in groups. There are lots of Mexican and Russian girls there by themselves. There are parts of town where we are not supposed to work. We only go there on our personal time, never working. Once when I was at the Nugget for a show I saw my protector arguing and shoving another man in front of the hotel. That night when Jose came to the house he was bleeding and bruised and went into a room with the others. Many of the people from our family came to the house that night, but they told us nothing," she said, her voice trembling somewhat.

"The next week I was going for my appointments and they gave me a small pistol to carry. They said not to be afraid to use it if I was bothered by anyone not wanting me there. We all carry small guns in our purses. Two of our sisters disappeared last month," she said sadly. "Jose is always close so if we have a problem, we call him and he is there right away."

"Can you give us your phone number so we can see you again?" asked Phillip.

"Sure. It is a cell phone and the call will be answered by my voice, but I will have to call you back. We are not supposed to answer in person." She talked to them while writing.

"Thank you Paula. Can we give you a lift home? Do you live close to this hotel?" Juan asked.

"No, No. I will call our driver. They come from Brazil also and will always see that we are picked up and delivered to appointments. Jose and Raphael are always near." She smiled at us as she spoke.

"Let us pay you for your time Paula. It was worth a lot to us to be able to talk to you." Ricky handed her several bills.

Juan left to take food to Baby and to be in the parking lot when Jose or Raphael arrived.

Paula left the table and headed to the parking lot with her phone in hand.

"So, now what?" asked Ricky.

"We'll call her later to see if she has more time for us. But right now we follow Paula's driver and see if we can get a trace on the owner from the license plate," Phillip said.

They got to Juan and their car just as the driver pulled in to pick up Paula.

"Let's see if we can get in behind him and not loose him in this traffic. People must be going to work all day here for Christ's sake," said Phillip. They did not get too far when the driver pulled into another hotel in the north strip area.

"Damn, he is going to drop Paula again," Phillip said.

"That's ok, we can still follow him when he leaves this lot," Ricky said. It only took a minute to drop her at the side entrance and he was off again to the east of town.

As they tailed him they became aware that they were driving by some very exclusive homes mostly concealed from the street by six to eight foot high landscaped walls and ornate security gates. The driver turned just next to the guardhouse into a private gated community. The gates swung open for him and then closed before they could get a view of what home he was headed towards.

"Call a realtor and see if there are houses for sale on this street," said Juan. "That's how I used to look at property I never thought I could own."

Juan currently owned a beautiful home on five acres in a gated estate community. He always knew he would one day own a magnificent house after his gym became successful. Part of his home was partitioned as a work out facility where he could provide personal training to his upscale clients. Juan was where he wanted to be in life.

"Great idea," said Phillip. Then they looked up the first realtor in the phone book at the service station.

Chapter Eight

It took an hour, but we were bathed, dressed, coifed and ready to meet our pimp.

"I so need a nap," said Lucy. "I don't even care if they stand me in a corner to sleep."

"Oh, so do I." said Mattie. "One hour of sleep last night was just not enough. These raccoon eyes are going to give my age away!"

I asked Boo how I looked and she smiled and said it was odd that I cared.

"It is odd, but for some reason I want to look good. In the event we are arrested or have our pictures taken for a mug book or even worse if they find us dead I want to look good!" I said laughing.

We huddled together as we walked into the main living area somewhat apprehensive about what we would fine. There were still girls sitting around and Danni, Josh and their father were playing cards with a fourth person who had not been present before. Flowers were set out everywhere and the air smelled of roses. Somewhere there was a meal being prepared as the fragrance of baking bread was mixed with the roses. My thoughts went to raspberry jam on hot bread; no concern for where I was or what would happen to me.

"Well, let's have a look at you. Did you find the accommodations workable?" Danni asked as my mind jetted back to my current situation.

"Very nice," we said and then began talking all at once again.

"We are not prostitutes and are not going to work for you now. We are only here because of an unfortunate situation on the way to Las Vegas that caused us to flee from our room leaving our clothes and our money and the police who were trying to help us identify the men who threw the dog out of the van and peed on us as we drove behind them." Mattie took in breath as she realized that she was rattling out about three sentences into one.

"We haven't seen or heard from the police since last night when they were sleeping in the room down the hall," Lucy added.

"They were going to watch out for us, but we heard gun fire outside our room and jumped out of the window and ran to our car hoping to get here and get lost. We didn't even get to take our dog. She is with the men and hopefully she is alright. We picked her up when the Mexicans threw her out of the van on the roadside." I was almost whispering.

With that we all began to cry and there was dead silence in the room.

"That's a lot to take in," Danni said, in a kind voice, "What about the Mexicans. Is that who was following you?"

"Yes, we think so. They stole Boo's trailer from her SUV. Someone killed a family in a nearby town and burned them in their travel trailer and they have that vehicle and probably Boo's little trailer. No one knows yet what kind of car or truck they stole," Mattie tried explaining. "The police said there were nineteen Mexicans in the van they seized and two were dead. The police thought they might need our trailer for another haul of people to Las Vegas."

"We saw the van in the parking lot of a diner on our way here, south of Primm. We flattened two of the tires on the van before going in hoping they could not follow us right away. After trying to talk to them, Boo stabbed one of them in his hand at their table. We were still really upset after they threw out Baby," Lucy said very fast.

They all looked up startled.

"Not a baby, that's what we named our dog!" she exclaimed.

"One, in the restaurant, was caught by the police. But the others got away," Lucy started to cry.

"They are probably looking for our car right now. We parked it over by the Golden Nugget on the top level of the parking garage," I said.

"So the peculiar clothes you were in really were not your working clothes?" asked Danni.

"Oh no, those were received as donations that we had for the women's shelter, but we were too embarrassed to give them to the ladies," I said. "Can you imagine someone actually wearing those dresses, for real?"

"Well, for a while I hoped I had some new family members, but perhaps you need to be reclassified," Danni said with a smile.

"The new clothes look nice," the father said speaking for the first time.

He was a very good looking man, reminding me of Carl Withers.

He introduced himself as Victor. He was a very light skinned black gentleman, maybe fifty, and partially concealing an empty holster under a cream colored leather jacket.

The other man at the card table spoke to us. "The men who are after you are men who are not going to be showing their faces in the public, for their own safety. It will make it hard for them to find you, because here in Las Vegas, they are wanted by almost everyone including the police. These men bring the undocumented to work in the city and they are very abusive to these people. They place their women in areas where the women not only service tourists, but after sex they have their men beat or murder the client for his car or whatever valuables he has in the hotel room. They get the wallet and call their home and threaten their family until they get more money from them. Some are Mexicans, but some are Russian as well. They are to be feared, but like I said, they cannot be looking for you in the open."

"I would like you to stay with us for a few days until we see what will unfold with these men, if you don't mind?" Victor stated more than asked. "It's not a bad place to be and you can use any of the amenities on the other two floors. We have an exercise facility, spa and a pool. We call out for food, but we have a wonderful kitchen where you can fix your own meals if you wish."

"Josh and I will go out to some other areas of Las Vegas and see what we can find out about your situation and the men looking for you," Danni said.

"If you call your friends, the police, I would appreciate your advising them you are alright, but please do not give the address of our home. Our girls are treated very well and I don't believe you would find one of them that would want to be anywhere else. There is no pressure to be here. Some of our girls are going to college, some between jobs or marriages. Some just do this best and like what they do. Like an artist, they get better and better and get paid very well for their work," Danni said.

"Maybe we could ask you what names you wish to be called and that would make it seem more familiar here for you," Victor suggested.

"I am Sissy, this is Boo, this is Lucy and Mattie," I said as I touched their newly clothed shoulders.

So there we sat, Lucy in the white satin top and black trousers, Boo in the white wrap top with black pleated slacks. Mattie and I, because we were the blonder ones, selected black tops with winter white slacks. It made no difference, the clothes, which were made in Canada, were to die for; hopefully not to die for this weekend.

It was ten o'clock. We heard the beautiful grandfather clock on the entry hall wall.

"Maybe you ladies would like to nap a little and then we can have lunch close to one o'clock." Danni suggested.

We looked at one another and I felt blessed by the suggestion and nodded an appreciative yes.

Sylvia showed us to another large room where there were sleeping areas separated by lovely roped curtains. I gently crept onto the sumptuous silk bedspread and placed my throbbing head on the down pillow. I don't think I was awake for longer than five minutes. I did not hear my friends talking and I was very thankful to the pawn shop owner for kicking us out of his store so we were on the block when Danni pulled around the corner.

Three hours later Sylvia came to the door and knocked gently.

"Lunch will be ready in about fifteen minutes." She spoke softly into the room.

"Thank you," I heard Lucy say. I stretched and tried to rouse myself from the best three hours of sleep I could remember. No melatonin, no tryptophan, no valium, just massive fatigue. Sliding off the bed my feet hit the soft carpet and we all rallied like aged cheerleaders and headed for the dining area following Sylvia's soft voice.

"Ladies," Victor said as we entered the dining area, "we have decided to have friends in tonight and enjoy some card playing, food, soft music and conversation."

This is where the fabulous aroma of bread had come from. A beautiful table was laid out in front of us and I realized I was starving.

"It will be fun," said Danni, "and all you have to do is have a good time."

I spoke almost too quickly, saying I would love that, so I could eat. Dressing up in fabulously expensive clothes, eating wonderful food that I would never have cooked at home, enjoying conversation from handsome strangers, now that's what vacation was all about.

Lucy and Mattie agreed.

Boo asked, "What will our purpose be at this function?"

"Well actually," said Danni, "you will be bait. By bait, I mean, I want others to know you are here and that may be what it takes to get the trash out in the open. I am fairly certain I know who is trying to silence you, but until I can be certain I want you here. You will be in good hands. These men are probably stumbling around Las Vegas possibly hurting our girls trying to find out where you are. Once they know you are in town they will no doubt try planning a strategy to get to you and we can probably help provide a remedy for their search. We will get you out in the open with our protection of course. We are not violent, but we are well armed. We share territories with another family on the east side and will have some of those gentlemen over tonight with a few of their ladies. You may enjoy talking with them, you may not. That's up to you. In a day or two we hope to have this ironed out and you can go on your way with new clothes and hopefully some new friends," Victor said.

Chapter Nine

The realtor Juan had phoned arrived right on time and was strangely attired in a long sleeve shirt, sweater vest and linen pants. It was an odd choice considering it was in the high seventies outside. He drove so slowly thru the development that it was hard to stifle yawns. Listening to him was painfully tedious but absolutely necessary if they wanted to locate Paula's driver's car.

"Do you want more than four bedrooms?" he asked as rolled through a stop sign.

"Five would be nice," said Phillip, "and if we could find a pool and territorial views that would be a real bonus."

"Oh, they all have pools. Some of the biggest money in the country resides here. There's golf on the west side of the development with fabulous sunsets and if you buy on the point there are sunrises too," he said to us from the front seat.

The houses were indeed magnificent Ricky thought. The yards reminded him of topiary he had seen in South Carolina at Bishopville. A man named Pearl had created fabulous yards for people to come visit. He wondered to himself if these people knew of him.

They passed houses with pink statuary in the yard. The realtor told them many of the yards were illuminated year round with white lights, intensifying the pink color and making it appear fleshy. Fences blocked views of most homes from the street, but many of the driveways did provide peek-a-boo view corridors and they all craned their necks in search of the driver's car.

And there, just as they were about to abandon their search, parked in a circular driveway beside a tiered waterfall was the car. Two lovely girls were getting into the car and the driver was closing the door as they were settled in comfortably. The car pulled from the opening gate and Juan quickly made note of the license plate and the street address.

"That's a nice place," Juan said, asking the realtor to stop.

"Oh yes, that's a very fine family from Central America. They have lived here for many years and always have relatives coming in and staying. That is one of the largest houses in the community. They have excellent views of the city skyline, the golf course and fabulous sunsets from the west side of the home. Beautiful place! I don't think there is a price you could offer that would entice them," the realtor said.

"Is there anything else on this street?" Ricky asked.

"There is a widow three doors down that I could call. She works with another agent in my firm and has been inquiring about one of the penthouses now available on the strip." Dollar signs were twinkling in his eyes.

"That would be wonderful. We do have another appointment in a short time, so we should let you go and retrieve that information," Ricky said. "Let me give you my cell phone number so you can let us know right away. We need to make this a short trip and finding something today or tomorrow would be ideal."

"Perfect," said the realtor as he drove them to their vehicle just outside the development gates.

"Let's get over to the Clark County sheriff's office and see what we can find out on the license plate," Ricky said.

"It amazes me how many people have moved to Las Vegas in the last couple of years. There seems to be more money here than some of the larger coastal cities," Juan observed.

"Well Trump and Wynn wouldn't be here if there wasn't money to be made."

The courthouse and sheriff's office were oddly lacking in parking space. They made three trips through the lot before using local police parking spots.

"It must be all the newlyweds," Juan joked.

"This is where I would do it next time," said Ricky. You have the entertainment, the vacation environment, the sexy clothes and great restaurants. What else do you want for those first few nights?"

"A good woman would be nice," said Phillip.

"Well, that goes without saying," said Ricky. I tried the other, believe me, a good woman would be nice."

The entered the crowded station walking directly to a receptionist station in the front.

"We would like to talk to the detective in charge," Ricky stated smiling at the receptionist which always helped.

"That would be O'Reilly. Let me give him a call," she said hiding a yogurt and wiping her mouth.

"O'Reilly, a nice Irish name," Juan said.

They waited in the lobby watching the people stack up in the marriage license line hugging and kissing and full of excitement. "What interesting combinations of people," Juan said.

"Gentlemen, how can I help you?" asked a large red haired muscular fellow with a very friendly smile and a booming voice. He had a bad scar on the right side of his face which kept his smile broader on the left.

After shaking hands, Ricky began explaining where they had come from and where they hoped to end their journey.

"The girls are still missing?" O'Reilly asked.

"Yes, they are. We called their cell phone and a man answered and said they were alright and hung up." Ricky told O'Reilly. "The number did not ring through when we called it back."

O'Reilly asked his receptionist for a list of any calls into the station in the last twelve hours that were or were not handled by his men.

"We fear the men trying to find them are the same ones that took their trailer, a small six foot by eight foot covered trailer with a large enclosed tool box. They clipped the electrical, removed the hitch and away they went. They may also be the ones that killed and burned a family that was camping outside of Victorville. They heisted the family's vehicle, but we are not certain of the make or model. We have no results yet on dental work for the family that was found at the campsite. The stolen vehicle must have a trailer hitch. The trailer where the deceased were found had no vehicle in the immediate area. The men looking for the women are Mexican. There were nineteen people in the van they were bringing this direction. Two were dead. They also threw a dog out of the van which the women picked up. That was the reason the women stopped at the restaurant where one of the women assaulted one of the men inside with a steak knife," Phillip said.

"What happened to the dog they threw out? Is it still alive?" asked O'Reilly. "I can't stand a bastard that abuses animals. I will put that son of a bitch in jail before a mugger anytime. They know it here too. If I get an animal abuse call I go in person. I enjoy treating them worse than they ever could an animal."

"Oh yes! We have Baby, that's the name they gave her, and we are treating her like a bar of gold. She means a lot to the women and we have grown extremely fond of her. We took a room at the Hilton Suites and that's where she is now. She needs to recuperate a little more. We'll pick her up shortly for an outing," Juan replied to O'Reilly.

"Well, I can get an APB out on any vehicles with small trailers in tow. I could have the girls go thru mug books, if you had the girls, but in this case I will have to go to my "sewer network" and find out where or who these men might be. I'll send out a couple of men to get any known information right now. We have some very reputable men in the city that would also be extremely upset by the prostitutes these transporters may have been bringing into Las Vegas. They give the profession a bad name if you know what I mean?" O'Reilly said.

O'Reilly's secretary came in with two open reports, one from a woman robbed in the Fashion Mall and one that was cut off in mid sentence from a women without a name or call back number.

"Do you have a license plate for the vehicle the women were driving?" asked O'Reilly. "I do," said Phillip. "It's a 2008 Cadillac SUV – Escalade plate number Blu-I's. We put those plates on the car in Primm. It's Dark Blue with a missing trailer hitch and high polished chrome wheels. The windows are tinted beyond the legal limit. It belongs to Florence, they call her Boo, Gemmell. Probably her husband is on the title too. I think his name is Joseph," Ricky said. "What they don't know is all of our police plates read Blu-I's."

"Joseph Gemmell, that name rings a bell. It will come to me," said O'Reilly, thinking those girls had a nice ride.

Chapter Ten

"We were damn lucky to find those campers since those fuckin police took our van. That trailer will come in mighty handy for the next pick-up," said Ruiz.

"Those meddlin bitches. Wait till I get my hands on them. I'm gonna keep em prisoners somewhere no one will ever look. Just keep em for myself like in a basement in an old abandoned house somewhere. Then someday one will want to marry me and I'll kill the others!" Huey, his partner said.

"Be sure she has one of them dowries. We could use the money stupid! Manny is not going to be happy when he hears bout this."

"Yeah, and that should be any minute. We were supposed to be in Las Vegas by midnight last night. He's out over forty grand for that truckload. We can get about eight to ten stuffed in that little trailer we stole, laying flat," Ruiz said.

"Yeah, but that's a move out, not a new batch comin into town. We were supposed to deliver the nineteen and pick-up twenty to take back south. Maybe we could find some little people to take back!" Huey laughed as he thought about what he'd said. Ruiz wasn't laughing.

"Shit, we're screwed. Let's make the call to him first and not wait for him to call us. I'd rather be on the phone with Manny than in person when we tell him what happened," Huey said.

"First, I wanna get the trailer cleaned out and throw away whatever is in the box and make as much room as possible. I'm thinking you might be right, twelve small people. Maybe we'll just move twelve whores to Reno. Manny's gonna want to know exactly what our plan is," Ruiz said trying to adjust the outside mirror.

"Well, let's pull this barge off the road. How do people afford gas for family trips? I'd make my damn kids work and pay for fuel. We can't buy gas and food, specially if Manny doesn't pay us soon," Huey babbled on.

"I don't see anybody behind us so let's pull over here and get that top off." Ruiz talked as he spit tobacco out the partially opened window. The truck slid into the gravel bringing a large cloud of dust over the vehicle.

Huey jumped out getting dust all over himself. "Get me a pry bar to get this box open. It's a good thing I'm so strong," Huey said throwing all his weight on the bar. "Jesus H, come look at this Ruiz! Holy Shit! It's a body!" Huey screamed to the Ruiz in the cab.

"What a smell!" Ruiz said holding his nose. "Turn it over. Is it a man or a woman?"

"Not me, you do it. Its' head has a hole in the back. It's a guy. Something hard hit his skull," Huey said, holding his breath.

"Or someone," Ruiz thought out loud.

"Here, pull on his jacket with the cane we found behind the seat. You really don't want to touch his skin with no glove," Huey said.

"Geez us Christ… It's Joe. He was supposed to be in Panama last week," Ruiz said to Huey who was gasping for air.

"Well if you thought Manny was going to be pissed about the van, this will bring him here screamin. That fat bastard's heart will stop. Joe is his best recruiter," Huey said to Ruiz.

"Here, you call him," Ruiz said passing the phone to Huey.

"No way, you do it. He thinks I would be happier dead. That's what he said last time he saw me. Actually, when he is around I would be happier dead," Huey said.

"He said he thought you would be less stupid if you were dead. I thought it was kind of funny!" Ruiz said to him, smiling. "Give me the god damn phone. My head hurts just thinking of this call."

Ruiz dialed. The phone rang five times and he hoped it would go to the answering machine, but no. Manny picked up and slurred, "This better be important."

"I know you weren't expecting this call, this is Ruiz, but things have gone to shit and I thought you would want to know first hand. We found Joe dead in a trailer that we stole. I know it is Joe, Manny," Ruiz said. "We opened this tool box and his body was in there. We stole the trailer to move some small whores (he stifled his laughter) out of Las Vegas because the police took our van and we just opened the lid and there he was, dead and stinking to high heaven."

He heard Manny sigh into the phone getting ready to talk, but he kept on with his story trying to make it sound better so Manny wouldn't kill them.

"It was four women traveling to Vegas that had that trailer. We came across them in a restaurant and for no reason they stabbed the hand of one of our best haulers named Leo, and then the police came and got two of our guys but Leo got away. The police got the van. We were damned lucky to get out of that van and get to the campground where we found a family camping. We took their truck cause it had the hitch on it and we left them there."

"Even if I was fucking drunk you would sound like an imbecile. Do you wanna try making sense before I hire someone to kill you?" Manny answered.

"The women in the restaurant ran into us earlier. The other hauler opened the van and pissed out the back and it got on their car."

"No, that wasn't all. Well, he threw a dog out that was getting sick in the van so it didn't stink so bad. It was one of those Doberman dogs. The women stopped and picked it up. That's why they were so pissed I guess."

"No, the family at the campground they found won't be reporting it missing. We left them there real dead. We changed the plates on the truck, so it'll take em awhile to find out what it looks like.

"No, they won't identify them people right away. We set em on fire."

"We can pick you up at any time you want sir. We can get rid of it right now. We'll go to the Lake Mojave area and fire it up. There should be nothing left. Yes sir, I know how to get there. Yes sir, and get back." Ruiz completed the conversation with a sweaty brow and disconnected the call.

"Asshole! He thinks I'm too stupid to find Lake Mojave. I'd like to have him in that trailer when it goes up," Ruiz said.

"Why don't you tell him that then?" Huey laughed.

"Because I wanna go on havin sex. He'd make sure that didn't happen," Ruiz said.

"He wants us to burn the trailer with Joe in it?" His partner asked.

"He says they'll trace Joe to us. He's so full of shit. He's gonna call when he gets in for us to pick him up," Ruiz said.

"Are we picking him up at the airport?" Huey questioned.

"I didn't ask that because then he'd think I was as stupid as you! He's flying in! How else would we get him, with a net?"

"How long will it take us to get to that Lake Mojave?" Huey asked.

"How the shit do I know? Let's go buy a map," Ruiz said lighting a cigarette he found in the ashtray with the car lighter. "These God damn people smoked when there were children in the car. They probably all had cancer anyway."

Chapter Eleven

"Did you run the license on the driver's car?" Ricky asked the front desk as they were leaving O'Reilly.

"We have a name and address for Raphael Sanchez. Here you go. It's a 2007 Cadillac right?" the clerk asked.

"Yeah." said Ricky.

"Look at this. It's the same as the house address where we saw him today. All the vehicles must be licensed through that house. How very clever. No one can just drop in on the drivers, because they wouldn't have individual addresses," Ricky said to Phillip and Juan.

"O'Reilly would know who owns that fabulous house. He seems to know almost everything about everyone here," Juan said to the others.

"Let's go back and ask him," said Phillip. "What's O'Reilly's first name?"

"The name on his desk plate says Shawn," said Juan.

Back in O'Reilly's office the three detectives found Shawn at his desk.

"Excuse me, Shawn, do you know this address?" Ricky asked the Irishman.

O'Reilly looked at the paper and smiled broadly. "Oh yes. This is one of the guys I was talking about when I said they'd make your trip to Vegas memorable. He's a good man, has a good congregation, so to speak. Actually I can take you to see him if you wish. He is very accommodating and I think you would enjoy seeing his automobile collection. It's been awhile since I visited with him. Shall I give him a call?" Shawn asked.

"Well, not the answer I expected," said Ricky, "but we would love to go and see what, if anything, he knows about our ladies in question."

"I'll join you in the lobby," said Shawn. "Have some coffee. I'll be right back."

Chapter Twelve

"I wouldn't pay four bucks for a map. You should a stole it or just asked that buck toothed girl the directions," Ruiz said.

"Let's look and see how long it'll take. This trailer smells like hot urine since the top was unscrewed," Huey said.

"Did you call that Mendez guy to find that SUV? He can locate any vehicle for resale real quick, I'm sure the asshole can find one to burn," Ruiz said.

"Yeah, I talked with him. He wants five large for the job," said Huey.

"Christ, now we're out forty-five grand," Ruiz was shaking his head in disgust as he spoke.

"Don't forget the map, four bucks more," laughed his partner.

"You laugh now, wait till Manny gets here. One smile and your lips will be gone. One word and your fat tongue will be next," Ruiz said.

"Better not pee in front of him, I guess," Huey said laughing.

"I can't find Mojave, how do you spell it?" asked his partner.

"Just like it sounds for Christ's sake," said Ruiz. "M-o-h-a-v-e."

"Let's take it to the Valley of Fire State Park. That sounds good, kinda like it was meant to be. Its close, just a little north of where we are now. I'm gonna say fifteen minutes. Let's see what the stereo sounds like. I always wanted one of these CD players. Maybe we should keep that girlie car if he finds it. I bet it smells nice and has nice sounding CDs." The music started and both frowned. "That's religious music. Turn it off. Those people deserved to die for listening to that."

"Are we there yet?" Ruiz asked Huey. "I have to piss."

"It should be right around this curve," Huey said. "Slow down, here is the dirt road showing on the map."

"Not a bad area," Ruiz said. "Let's back it in here and get it off the hitch. We haven't passed anyone for five minutes." Crossing a small broken culvert they were quickly off the road and into an area concealed from any oncoming traffic. "Get the gasoline."

"I'm gonna piss along side of the trailer, just give me a minute," Huey said.

"There's a shitter over there, you could use it."

"No way," he said relieving himself as he talked. "Probably has those killer spiders inside."

"Hurry, just get a lot of gas on him. Manny doesn't want any identification made. That would piss him off more if there's any pissin room left. He wants nothin left to trace."

"Do we have matches?"

"Christ, no," Ruiz said. "I'll heat up the cigarette lighter, use it. We just lost trade-in value if we trade this boat in! Here catch! Let's get the Hell out of here."

"Ouch, that's hot! Where did it go? Wait, I have gas on my foot. Shit, the fire is on my pants! Should I get the lighter back?"

"Kick off them pants and get in the goddamn car. We gotta get away from here! Forget the lighter." Huey jumped in the truck.

"There goes Joe," his partner said. "Wow, what a fucking explosion! There won't be anything left of him. Oh shit Ruiz, it's catching that brush where my pants landed over by the outhouse! Floor this beasty truck buddy, this looks like it might be a little bigger barbeque than planned!"

"Don't turn around shithead. The less we know about this the better. That tumbleweed was dryer than I thought."

"Do you think?"

Taking a peek back they shouted, "There goes the outhouse!"

Both knew, as they sped away, what they weren't turning to see was going to be a catastrophe.

"Where's your god damn underwear?" Ruiz said as he noticed Huey was sitting with his privates facing him in the front seat.

"I didn't put em on this morning," he said.

"Christ, I'm not looking at that one minute more. Put those stinkin swim trunks on we found in the back seat!"

"I never wear them plaid color shorts. I hope he don't have no crotch disease," Huey said as he struggled to get into the plaid pants.

They were laughing so hard they failed to notice the black clouds of smoke rising into the sky that were reflecting in the rear view mirror.

Chapter Thirteen

"How are the plans coming for this evening's gathering?" Victor asked.

"Everything looks in order. The food will be delivered by four o'clock and the piano man is coming at five o'clock," Sylvia smiled at him in reply.

"Will Garcia be bringing family and guests?" Danni asked.

"Yes and I might add they were very pleased and looking forward to the evening. He is bringing a case of your favorite scotch. I didn't think to ask what that was, knowing you would appreciate the thoughtfulness regardless."

"Excellent! We need to connect more with his family. Garcia showed a lot of class when those Russian bastards wanted to come into our area and partner with him," Victor said. "I heard there were some broken bones when Garcia's boys finished with those men."

"The Russians probably moved to the south side," said Danni, "but we didn't have to utter a word. We owe one to Garcia for that."

"How are our four ladies doing? I hated to call them bait, but it will be to their benefit for us to find these people before they find the girls," Victor told his boys.

"Shawn O'Reilly is meeting with Garcia today. I just had a call from headquarters," Danni told Victor and Josh.

"Will you call Garcia and ask that he bring Shawn tonight? There's another person we need to massage a little more," Victor said to Sylvia, touching her hand as she left.

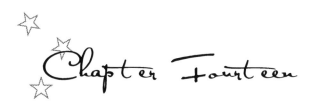

Chapter Fourteen

Shawn arrived at Garcia's place around three o'clock with Ricky, Philip and Juan in tow.

Garcia was expecting them and offered them a hardy handshake and a cold beverage leading them through the house to a brightly colored covered patio overlooking the golf course.

The magnificent furniture and architecture of the home were overwhelming. There were many hallways exiting the entry foyer as they passed through and a staircase reaching for the sky with open skylights showing the passing clouds.

"It's my version of the Bellagio ceiling with clouds moving and a multitude of bright stars at night," said Garcia.

"It is awesome!" said Juan. He so loved art, design and architecture. "The curved beams must be the support for those windows. They look like they would need beams that size. Are they from the hull of a large ship?"

"Yes, they were made in Brazil. It wasn't easy finding support beams that could be shaped for the staircase radius. I am a fortunate man to have all life has given me. I am truly blessed," Garcia said, holding his cigar away from his lips.

They sat in the courtyard soaking up the perfect seventy-five degree day and drinking in the smells of the freshly cut grass from the golf course.

"I told my friends from Ontario that we might possibly have a look at your automobile collection?" Shawn suggested to Garcia.

"Of course, and I have a couple new ones from the Scottsdale auction last month. They were practically giving cars away. I drove home the Ferrari." Garcia smiled.

It took about forty-five minutes to view the collection of autos in the altered daylight basement of the home. The entry was from a private drive leading into a colorfully tiled floor with mosaic walls and fifteen fabulous collector vehicles polished with no where to go.

"I'll take one out every once in a while, but there is a little problem with auto theft in this city so leaving them unattended is a risk. Shawn has to work on that a little harder," Garcia laughed.

"What brings you to see me my friend? It's been some time," Garcia asked.

"These gentlemen have missing women issues and I thought if anyone could help or has heard anything it would be yourself or possibly Victor," Shawn said.

"It's odd that you would mention him, Shawn. He asked that I attend an event at his home tonight and I mentioned you were coming to see me today. He then asked that I invite you to attend with me. Some cards, some updating, a lot of food; you know the program. He even has calypso music coming in for atmosphere," Garcia said.

"I would be honored," said Shawn. "It's been a long time since we've all been together."

"We are looking for four women that are trying to escape from none other than Manny's boys. This is my thought, but I think someone was running Mexicans in when these women turned them in to the police for inappropriate behavior and animal abuse. The women are not very popular, because by turning them in the police in turn found nineteen men and women crammed into a van headed to Vegas. This was in Victorville yesterday. One of the men was pinned to a restaurant table with a steak knife by one of the now missing women. He escaped custody by ripping his hand loose, and two others got away from the van, possibly three, and then caused more fatalities by stealing a vehicle after killing the owners," Shawn told Garcia.

"They also stole a trailer that was attached to the women's SUV. We're thinking they're planning to use the trailer to haul more people since their van was confiscated by the authorities. We also suspect they're not stopping with the trailer. They want the women who can identify them," Ricky said.

"Manny won't be pleased when he gets wind of this screw-up. He's probably heard the news by now, so we better move fast before they find the girls," Shawn said.

"Manny," said Garcia, "what a piece of shit. He should have been put away long ago. He is like a bad smell that just spreads and spreads. He has no regard for life, his or anyone else's. That greasy little bastard has had his nine lives."

"I have heard nothing about these women. I will make a couple of calls and when I see you later today I can give you any information I find," Garcia said, shaking his head.

"Thank you Garcia. It's always an honor and a pleasure to be in your home." With that Shawn turned to Ricky as a gesture for them to leave.

At that moment, Paula came thru the lobby and stopped to look at Ricky. She glanced at Phillip and Juan, smiled and kept going thru the room.

"Lovely girl," said Ricky.

"She's a star. Let's ask her. If you want to know about anyone new in Vegas, ask the girls," Garcia said with a smile on his face.

"Paula, these are friends of mine from outside town visiting with Mr. O'Reilly. They are looking for four friends, women that would be new to town in just the last day or so. Any talk going on?"

"Perhaps one of the girls working in the North End spoke of new women on the block by the Nugget last night. They were Danni's girls. That's all I heard sir."

"Thank you Paula," Garcia said and she was off.

"Thank you for asking. That actually might be a useful clue." Ricky realized they really had no new information, but the new prospects were making him feel a bit more upbeat. He felt happier as they headed for the car.

"We need to get Baby and take her for a ride. Shawn, we'd appreciate your keeping in touch with us. You have our cell phone numbers, anytime is a good time. We won't be sleeping until this has been resolved." Ricky, Juan and Phillip parted.

"Thank you, by the way, for the visit to Garcia's home, it's quite a stunner. It's easy to see that you two are close friends and I respect that. Bottom line, a job is a job and if you can make everyone happy, then it's a great job." Phillip shook Shawn's hand as they parted, anxious to get back to their car.

"Now that's a house I could come home to after work," said Ricky, as they drove from the home.

"I could work in that house all day and still be glad to be there," said Phillip.

"I would settle for relatives that lived there so I could visit," laughed Juan.

Ricky, Phillip and Juan headed for the Hilton to freshen up and get Baby for a walk and a ride. They were amazed about how many people asked about the dog's well being. They were good people.

Ricky, Phillip and Juan had just gotten to their room, turned on the TV and sat down for a cold beer, when the news flashed on the TV about a wildfire in the national park.

"There is considerable smoke filling the sky from the National Park area and the FAA has issued a class 2 visibility warning to aircraft. Only limited commercial flights are being permitted to land or depart when breaks appear in the thick blanket of smoke... No further reports on the cause of the fire are available, but people are cautioned to stay out of the area for the next few hours. If fire intensity increases an evacuation alert may be issued. Stay tuned to Channel 7 for updates on the hour."

"What a place!" Juan said. "There's never a dull moment or lack of activity."

Baby came over and put her head on Ricky's knee. He looked at her and said, "Yes, I love you too and I miss the girls. We will find them, I promise."

It was three-thirty and time to take a walk with Baby until Shawn got back to them. They liked Shawn. He seemed to be in charge of the situation and obviously knew the right people in the city. He would be a good contact and possibly a good friend in the future.

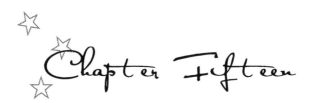

Chapter Fifteen

Boo was doing some stretches in the spa while Lucy and Mattie hit the free weights. I had decided to have a full body massage and was feeling like I might like to move in for an extended stay. I wondered what I could do in lieu of sex to get a full time position here with Sylvia. I'd like a job like Sylvia's, where people came to me for advice and I just bought things. That would be ideal.

Following my session, which turned out to be a shiatsu massage, with a very enthusiastic masseuse who had kneaded and stretched my tender muscles, I shuffled down to see my friends in my big fluffy slippers. The masseuse had produced a whole new framework of throbbing pain, arguably worst than that I had previously been tolerating, but I knew it would take away the original pain in time.

"Did you look at the selection of clothes we have for this evening?" Mattie asked. They were pouring through the racks of clothing.

"They are beyond fabulous. Most of them were made by European and Canadian manufacturers. I have one garment at home from one of these labels. It was a gift to myself last year," Lucy replied.

"I am anxious to meet some of the women who do work for Danni and his family tonight. This would be a nice place to visit if we actually had new friends," I said.

"I hope our police escorts are not worrying themselves into an early grave," said Mattie. "I feel somewhat guilty about being this well taken care of when they must be thinking the worst. I need to call their headquarters because the only private phone number I had is on my lost phone."

"I wonder if they found our purses back in our room at Primm? It certainly would be easier than calling the credit card companies to cancel and getting another good drivers license picture," laughed Lucy. "It took me three tries to get the one I have."

"I am definitely going to change to this make-up if we ever get home." My mind was jumping from one new experience to another like a child loose in a candy store.

"Sylvia looks like someone who would make these selections. What a job. Buy everything beautiful, be around good looking men all day and not be obligated for sex, unless you wanted it, of course," said Boo.

We laughed and continued on with our rest and relaxation for another hour.

Chapter Sixteen

Lying on a cheap, lumpy, stained mattress, Ruiz told his partner to pass him another beer from the cooler. It wasn't cold, but it was where the beer was located.

"You don't want to be drunk when Manny calls from the airport," Huey said.

"Fuck Manny!" Ruiz said. "I'm a little sick of his fucking attitude. He needs a lethal injection!"

The phone rang just as he finished his sentence.

"Ruiz? It's Manny. Pick me up at building B, departure level, not baggage level. Do you understand the difference? Two o'clock."

"Of course I do sir," Ruiz said giving the phone the finger.

"Glad you got here sir. I thought you might be earlier, but I'm glad you finally landed," Ruiz said with his eyes crossing at his partner.

"Well, some asshole started a fire in the national park and we had to circle until the smoke cleared enough to land," he said hanging up.

"Did you just give the finger to the phone?" asked Huey. Why is your mouth making that funny shape?"

"Turn on the news," Ruiz shouted to his partner.

"*….and at this time, 500 acres of the national park is engulfed by the fire. The burn area is now 50% contained and the fire marshal* *expects to have the entire fire under control within the next few hours pending wind conditions."*

"Turn it off!" he yelled.

"Do you think?" his partner began.

"Gee, do you think!" Ruiz said sarcastically.

"Let's get our asses to the airport," Ruiz said. "We need to get him at the departure level. Do you know which is which? We'll just drive around until we see his stumpy little body and big cigar. He wishes his dick was as big as his cigar I think!"

"Were we supposed to get Manny a room somewhere?" Huey asked Ruiz.

"He didn't ask," Ruiz said. "We couldn't afford the room. He doesn't stay where we do."

They washed their faces with cold water and, lacking any hand towels, dried with the dirty curtain that was hung close by the sink. Both farted in unison, surprising each other, and laughed as if they were watching a funny movie as they left the "palatial" motel room for the airport.

His partner asked as they drove to the airport, "Ruiz, do you ever wonder what the (**H**) stands for in Jesus **H** or the (**A**) in fucking **A**?"

"All the time," Ruiz said. "All the fucking time."

Chapter Seventeen

Ricky, Phillip and Juan took Baby and headed for the north side of town. They went down Bonneville and parked the car on the south side of the Fremont Street arcade. Behind the hotels they felt they could let Baby find a place to stretch and get rid of the days food and water.

She jumped out of the car with the twenty foot leash keeping her close enough so no harm would come to her. She sniffed around a little, and finally relieved herself looking a lot happier. What a wonderful dog she was to watch over. No problems in the hotel room where she had been waiting for hours. Baby knew she was to wait. Someone had trained her well. Her owner had to be one of the dead men or the returned aliens from the van. If one of the runners owned her there would have been fight marks or scars from abuse on her face or body.

Baby's ears suddenly went up and she seemed to sniff the air in the direction of the Nugget. Ricky let her have her leash and followed. As they got to the parking lot she began to whine and wanted to enter the parking lot.

"Follow her closely," Phillip said. "She wouldn't care if there was danger if the girls' scent is detected."

Up one floor, up two floors, up to the top floor and there was the SUV. Baby ran to it and put her feet up on the driver's door, whining to get in.

"Come on Baby, we can wait on this for a short time." They looked in the windows and saw nothing. No blood, thank God. They were out there somewhere and they had to find them.

"Let's go. We'll come back soon," Ricky said.

They turned and using the stairs next to the SUV, headed down to the street level.

As they reached the second floor there was a loud explosion from the floor above and miscellaneous large pieces of debris from the SUV flew over the side of the garage, crashing on the street below.

"What the hell?" Ricky shouted.

They rushed back up to the top floor using the exit ramp but there was no sign of the SUV they had just left. Instead, the spot where it had been parked only a few minutes ago was now charred black leaving only a large section of the still burning car frame and the smoking seats that had apparently ricocheted off the parking structure wall into an adjacent parking stall.

"Jesus Christ," Juan said. "Is God with us today or what? I'm sure glad we didn't stop to go through the vehicle!"

"I don't hear tires screeching or anyone running. It must have been detonated by remote control or a timer. Someone was probably just here wiring it as we were coming up and they were likely long gone by the time we got down to the second floor. And I thought no one had any idea that we were even here. Christ!" Ricky said.

"That's optimistic," said Juan. "They probably didn't give a shit and it was the evidence they were getting rid of, not us."

"Let's get down to the main street to see if anyone is standing around admiring his work," Philip said.

Scanning the street below from the third floor revealed that there were lots of people gathering across the street after hearing the explosion. "All those characters look suspicious. How do you detect a guilty guy from that motley assortment of tourists, transients, street people and other, hung over, oddly dressed people? Welcome to Las Vegas" Juan said.

When they reached the ground level, Baby began whining again and pulled the leash tight, heading toward the pawn shop.

They let her lead them to the front door where she stood up against the glass front door on her hind legs, scratching to get in.

They encountered a small Asian man reading a Chinese print newspaper at the counter as they entered.

"Have you been here all day?" Phillip asked.

"I here twenty hours each day, every day, fifty-two weeks a year. No one taking my business from me!" the man shouted back.

"A year, a year," the parrot screeched.

"We're not here to take your business; we're here to ask you some questions about four missing women. Our dog seems to have picked up their scent which makes us think they were here," Juan said.

"Missing women, missing women," said the parrot.

They looked at the parrot.

"I knew they were trouble. They were filthy whores and want money from me to get room. I say no, get out. I told them I call police if they not get out. They had no purses and they dressed ugly."

"Whores, whores, ugly, ugly," repeated the parrot.

"Do you know where they went, which direction?" Ricky asked wanting to choke the stupid son-of-a-bitch.

"No, I say go, you not working outside my shop. I showed them my gun, they left in hurry. They whores. I want no trouble from the police." The shop owner was becoming edgy and his face had started to sweat profusely.

"Police, police, whores, whores." The parrot would not shut up.

"We are the police. We want to find those women. They were not whores. They needed help. They may have slept on the street because of you. They may be dead," Ricky shouted menacingly.

"Whores, dead, whores," the parrot went on.

"When we find them and if they are hurt, we will be back. Trust me, you will know their pain you son-of-a-bitch," Phillip cursed toward him.

"Bitch, whores," said the parrot as they left.

Baby stretched up to nip the noisy parrot, but Ricky pulled her back.

"Good idea," Ricky said to Baby, "but not now."

As they turned to leave the pawn shop Baby pulled loose from her leash, hurled herself like a cannon ball and knocked the parrot stand over, causing it to crash onto the glass counter and sending the parrot and the contents of the glass case in all directions.

"Screeeeeeech!" We looked as the parrot landed on another counter top.

"Good girl," Ricky said softly.

The pawn shop owner started yelling in a garbled singsong frenzy, unrecognizable to the three police.

"Christ, I hate that man," said Phillip. "How could you mistake those four for whores? They look quite the opposite."

"Hey, Hey!" the pawn shop owner was running after them. "Here on phone, a picture of the whores and I want money for dog jumping."

They looked at the viewfinder and quit breathing. What in God's name were they wearing? Actually they looked kind of sexy, kind of like hookers, but where did that garbage come from?

"Give us that phone," Ricky demanded. "It will be returned to you after the girls are found."

"No, no, my phone. I give her ten dollar for this." He pulled the phone back.

Phillip and Juan grabbed the little man's arm and Ricky took the phone.

"I said it will be returned. It's evidence that you didn't kill them, ok?"

"I knew they trouble," he muttered as he backed away. "Whores!"

"Christ, Ricky," said Phillip. "I can only imagine the hell they must be going through right now. No money, no clothes, no food. I hope they are not hurt lying in a ditch somewhere trying to stay safe and out of sight. We should call the hospitals in the area, perhaps they went there for protection."

"I will take them to the best spa in town when we find them," Phillip said wringing his hands.

Baby continued pulling them down the sidewalk as she smelled the cement. She ended, whining at the curb, still looking for a place to continue, but no other scent to follow.

They looked at Baby and then at each other, forlorn, despair on their faces.

"Now what?" they said together. "Perhaps they were taken in a car at this point?"

"Why would they part with one of their phones?" Ricky shrugged, "unless they needed money for something to eat."

Chapter Eighteen

"I don't think I have ever looked better," I said.

"Or felt better," Boo said.

Lucy and Mattie were finishing their hair and looked smashing.

It was nice being taken care of like this. Bait had a pretty good life. I was wondering if I could be bait again after this was over, if this got over.

It was five o'clock and we stepped out of our room down the hall from the living area. Several people were there already. Everything looked exquisite with the tables set up for cards and the rose colored curtained food tables interspersed with large floral arrangements separating the room into individual vignettes.

Some striking girls were standing around waiting to be dealers or hostesses as the evening came alive. Scantily clad, large and small breasted temptresses, all in black and white, moving everywhere with trays of cigars and liquor glasses glistening with ice and scotch moved among the guests. They would be receiving more in tips than a good business night on the street.

"I wonder if there will be drugs served this evening," I asked Boo.

"I wonder, but I would say no. It looks like a meeting where intelligence is expected. These do not look like drug users," Lucy said.

"Ladies," Danni called out. "You look wonderful. You look like my girls. I think if you change your mind you could do quite well!" he smiled. "Let me introduce you to some gentlemen who have your well being in mind."

He walked us to a table occupied by a very handsome man in a white linen jacket and dark blue trousers, an extremely muscular red haired gentleman, and two Latin looking men with more teeth than I had ever seen. They all stood.

My heart was racing. I hoped my friends felt the same way and I wasn't being slutty alone. Why weren't these men the ones who were chasing us? I would have made myself more available. I felt my face flush hoping they were not aware of my thoughts.

"This gentleman is Garcia. He has a vested interest in the business of the city and it angers him to think that we are being lessened in value by the likes of those looking for you. He has witnessed this for years and now at its pinnacle it must be addressed," Danni said as he introduced him.

"How very nice to meet you," Garcia smiled. "It is my pleasure to be in your life at this time."

In my life I thought. I did not remember my ex husband ever saying that to me. Not in that tone. He would say *"why in the hell are you in my life"*, but that was not the same. I would have kept him if he had spoken those words in the tender tone. I could build a lifetime around those words. What made a voice project like that? I was having standing sex I thought, although it had been awhile. But I also felt that way when I was near Ricky in the hotel. I am definitely a fantasy whore!

"Let me go thru these lovely ladies by name Garcia. This is Lucy, Mattie, Boo-which is short for Florence, and Sissy," Victor said.

He introduced the two Latin looking men at the table as Garcia's family, his younger brothers. He further said they were at our disposal. I secretly wished he would quit saying those things. Knowing Mattie, Lucy and Boo as I did, I knew we shared that subliminal thought; new lingerie, perfume, new bedding. Whew! I had to get serious about our situation.

"And this is Shawn O'Reilly. He is our police chief and has a very sincere interest in your story. He is also an animal lover and took an immediate interest in your saving the Doberman," Victor said.

"I believe you are very much missed by the police from Ontario. I spoke with them today and they will be delighted to know that you are safe and in very luxurious surroundings," Shawn said.

"They are alive?" we said together.

"Oh yes. It seems they were gassed in the hotel room and by the time they were brought to, you had gone, long gone actually. They were out for hours," Shawn said.

"What about Baby?" I said.

"She is very well and being treated like a queen, I am told. Those men do seem to love her as much as you all do. It was a good plan for them to keep her at the hotel in Primm. I don't know if Danni would have picked up women with a guard dog!" he smiled over at Danni as he spoke.

Tears came to our eyes and we felt a bit embarrassed.

"We hope to end this situation very soon," Shawn said, "and you will be together again."

"It's very nice to meet all of you. We truly appreciate your helping us." We walked away and they sat once again.

"I did not know men still stood to be introduced," said Lucy.

"I thought they only stood to shake their crotch out," Mattie laughed.

"I have such a feeling of relief, I think I am going to faint," Lucy said.

"Let's go talk to some of the girls. There's the one that was on the corner when Danni picked us up."

As we mingled with the other women I felt a sense of belonging. It was a similar feeling I had experienced around the women in the shelter in San Diego. These women, however, seemed to have everything they wanted or needed right now in their lives.

The cute little girl with the auburn hair that had talked with Lucy on the street corner came to us. She was excited to know if we would be staying and working with the family. It almost saddened me to say "no." She rejoined her friends after inviting us to have dinner with them later in the week.

We proceeded to meet all the people we could before the occasion was over. These could be our friends forever. I looked for Sylvia to thank her for everything she had done. She stood by a window in a simple single shoulder pink gown which hugged her fabulous curves and looked like cotton candy against her light brown skin. She had long pink earrings which caught the light and seeing us she smiled, opening her arms in a sign of welcome. She walked away from Victor toward us.

Chapter Nineteen

Shawn got a call while playing poker and had to excuse himself to talk.

"Mr. O'Reilly?" a small male voice came through the phone line.

"Yes, yes, who is this?"

"This is Mouse," he said. "I'm at the airport, where I usually hang out playing my guitar and I see that Manny fellow in the lobby by the United Airline door. He has on a pink shirt and white pants and sandals. Nobody has picked him up yet."

"Keep an eye on him Mouse and call me the minute you see him get into a car. Let me know what the car looks like and if you can get a license. Thanks."

Back at the table Shawn was all too happy to share his conversation with Garcia and Victor.

"Well," Victor said, "this must be a big deal for that worthless scrap of fat to come this far to get these women, if in fact that's what he is after this time. We might have to take the women out for a showing tonight."

"Mouse will call when they are picked up and we'll know what to look for on the strip. I'm sending a couple of cars to the airport to catch a tail. Did anyone win that hand?" Shawn asked.

Danni's phone rang and his informant said there was an explosion in the garage at the Nugget. They didn't know who or what was blown up, but it was on the third floor. There would be a news story coming up soon on channel nine.

Putting down the phone Danni walked to me and asked if we had parked the SUV at the Nugget garage third floor.

"Yes, in the corner space by the south stairs. Is someone going to pick it up?"

"More or less. Someone may have blown it up, so I think they will be picking it up!" Danni said.

"Boo, someone has blown up your car! I am so sorry," I said as I hugged her.

"Well," she said, "if Joe paid the insurance I have nothing to worry about. That makes the trailer and the SUV gone in two short days."

"We could not have planned a worse outcome for you on this trip," I said, knowing only part of it was bad.

"Everything will work out," Boo said. "Life is not always predictable."

Shawn walked over to Boo and asked, "Does your husband work in San Diego?"

"He works out of our house," she said. "He imports primarily, but also some exporting. He has done that for some time. Even before we were married."

"I can't help but think I know that name, Joseph Gemmell. It seems so familiar." Shawn scratched his curly red hair. "Do you carry a photo of the two of you?"

"Oh no," she said. "I tore it up once when I was angry. I don't think he would have been to Las Vegas. He always said he hated gambling and whoring. He would never bring me here. That's one of a hundred reasons I could hardly wait to come with my friends. It has turned out somewhat different as vacations go, but not worse than, actually better than," she said, smiling and still holding my hand.

The big screen was turned on in the den area and Sylvia came to tell Victor the news that was now showing.

Several of the men went into the den and watched the blast footage captured by the garage cameras. They also saw two hooded men setting the bomb and then the three policemen standing next to the SUV, probably just before it blew. Standing on the street, in the next sequence of footage, Shawn noticed Ricky, Phillip and Juan with Baby heading around the corner. So they knew that much already. That was good. They could be more aware of the caliber of the men out there and what they had in mind.

Shawn needed to call them and let them know the girls were safe right now.

Shawn's phone rang just then and Mouse was on the other end.

"Mr. O'Reilly, this is Mouse. There are two men with that Manny character. They look very tired and stupid and drive a red GMC SUV with Colorado plates. I couldn't get a number. They parked too close to the car behind them blocking the plate. They were in front of the departure area. They threw me a quarter for my guitar playing, cheap rat faced bastards."

"We will add to that Mouse, don't worry, and thanks," Shawn said.

Shawn went to Victor and Garcia. "Manny is with two idiots in the stolen GMC SUV. It has Colorado plates, red in color."

Chapter Twenty

Manny was not happy as he threw himself into the red SUV. His clothes were wrinkled and he was sweating profusely.

"Where did this vehicle come from?" He snapped, thinking his brother in law had the same vehicle.

"This is the one we stole from the campground outside of Victorville. We needed a van, this had a hitch and we knew where we could get a trailer to haul some ass from Vegas," said Ruiz.

"You were supposed to be bringing people in and then taking the same number out," Manny snapped. "What happened to those Mexicans that were in the van?"

"The police have them. Two were dead. The other 17 are somewhere with the police."

"How many were women?" Manny asked.

"Only six and they were ok. We made sure to take good care to have them women at the back where there was more air and we gave them more water too," Huey said.

"But that's not doing us any good where they currently ended up is it?" Manny said.

"No sir, but we thought we would haul some fresh girls to Reno in that trailer we stole, but then you told us to trash it with Joe in it so no one would know it was him," Ruiz said.

"Where did you take it? Please give me a satisfactory answer or I swear I will kill you both right here," Manny snorted.

"Shit, yeah, we did a good job. We took the trailer with smelly Joe and drove it to a park area outside town and set it on fire. We saw it burning when we drove away. No one was in that deserted park, no cars and no people. We checked it out first, sir," Ruiz said.

"Did you drive back by to see if there was anything left after you torched it?" Manny asked.

"No sir," said Huey, "that's where this really funny thing happened. We couldn't do nothin like that because we saw on the news there was a big fire in the same area and people were warned to stay clear for several hours, until the news said it was ok to go there again. We were lucky to get out of there before that crazy fire got us. We think it was already burning and we just added to it a bit from where we put smelly Joe."

Manny had his face covered with his beefy little fingers and he was breathing deeply as he asked, "Are you the nitwit bastards that started the fire everyone in the plane could see from the air? The fire and smoke that had the planes backed up for an hour circling this whore of a city?"

"Well, we seen that too on the news, but we don't know for sure nothin yet. It was in the same area where we burned Joe up, that's for shittin sure," said the partner. "Could you see flames from the air? I bet that was real pretty."

Manny rolled the window down and spit out the end of a cigar. He wanted to blow the head off Ruiz's shit head of a partner, but he would wait for that until he no longer needed whatever protection he might be able to give.

"Give me the god damn lighter," he snapped.

Only Ruiz's eyes looked sideways at his partner. "Where's the lighter?" he asked.

"Don't know. Must not of had one," he said. He turned his face away. It was flushing. He knew what was left of it was still at the fire site.

"Drop me at the Wynn. Don't get out, just go wherever it is you go to be stupid and I'll call you in an hour. I need to get some people together for tonight," said Manny.

How did these men come to be his? They were beyond imbeciles Manny thought.

"Oh yeah, and we had to promise that bossy asshole five thousand dollars to have that god damn car of those women blowed up. We didn't want them getting away again and it's all done, we saw that on the TV too. There was car parts all over the street." said Ruiz. "They was like roman candles."

"How many people were killed in that explosion?" Manny thought he said to himself.

"Oh none, we don't think. They didn't report that on TV," Huey said.

"Which door do ya want at the Wynn?" asked Ruiz.

"Does it matter? Why not the front entrance where reservations customarily are located?" Manny said sarcastically. Killing these two would be one of his happiest moments. He'd have a well earned celebration of relief after that deed was done.

"Do you want me to get your bag sir?" said Huey.

"No, I will handle that myself, without causing a scene or killing anyone. Just get the hell away. And take a shower before we meet tonight!"

They drove out bouncing from speed bump to speed bump keeping up their speed so it was more fun.

"He sure isn't very appreciative," Huey said. "I'm going to give him the finger when I think he can't see me. My mom used to say I had no promise in life, but I promise I'm going to hurt him one day."

Ruiz and his partner went to the motel and poured a couple of drinks of warm whiskey. They still had polish sausage and rye bread and some shrimp salad from a couple days earlier so they proceeded to construct the biggest sandwiches they could from the fixings, and then wolfed them down in great gulps like starving animals. They burped loudly and stretched out on the bed to relax, putting quarters in the massage machine to shake up the lunch a bit and aid their digestion. When the quarters ran out after thirty minutes they just curled up, exhausted but with bellies full, and dozed off for a midday nap.

Chapter Twenty-One

"I'm surprised Shawn hasn't called yet. I don't know where to go at this point. We know they are alive, poorly dressed, have no car to escape in and can only assume they have food and shelter," Ricky said with sadness in his voice.

"Shit, this has been a long day," said Phillip. "I think Mattie has the prettiest eyes and she looked damn nice in her hooker outfit."

"Great," said Juan. "Our boy's in love for the first time with a lost girl, dressed like a two dollar hooker, and doesn't know if he'll ever see her again."

"*Authorities now suspect arson at Valley of Fire National Park. Considered a crime scene at this point, no one is allowed to enter the area other than police and fire officials,*" the newscaster cut in.

"Well, that about pegs my excitement meter for today! Good God, what type of crime scene will this be? Well, we are police and we can get in there so let's go," Ricky said shaking his head.

"Baby, you stay here and be safe," said Phillip. "Apologizing for your loss would be impossible." Hoping Shawn was watching the television at this same time, they headed for the Park.

Chapter Twenty-Two

"Victor," Sylvia said in her honey sweet voice. "I believe you might want to watch the news on the fire north of town."

Again the men went to the den and listened as the announcer was warning the public they could not enter the national park because of the suspicion of a crime having been committed there.

"My God," said Shawn. "I know these are connected, but how?"

"I must leave you early Victor and get out there and see what's going on. I don't need to tell you that all hell is going to break loose tonight with Manny in town, explosions, fires and a full moon. We will be up to our asses in activity."

"I'll find out where Manny is staying. We will start from the most expensive hotels and work our way down," Victor said. "Between Garcia and me we should be able to get that info in no time."

"Keep me posted. That sleaze ball will make a mistake tonight and with luck we will be there to watch him fall," Shawn said.

"I'll have the hotel rep call you direct," Victor said as he patted his shoulder. "It is long past time for that bastard to be put in the ground. He's been fucking us for some time."

"He flies under the radar. He has those slimy little shits doing the visible work so they get their asses pinched while he skates on by collecting the money. Last month when that trailer of cooked immigrants was found in the parking garage of the convention center his name was all over it, but no one could attach a name to the stolen truck. He lost some big money that week and it looks like he is losing again this week, so he will be pissed." Shawn left the party.

Ricky's phone rang. It was Shawn. "Hello, Ricky?"

"Yeah, this is Ricky."

"Have you been watching the television at all?"

"Yeah, we're on our way to the fire scene. They said only police and firemen were allowed in the area. That was like an open invitation. What did you find out about the girls?" Ricky questioned him half heartily.

"Good news, Ricky. The girls are perfectly safe and being well taken care of at a friend's penthouse. They are actually classified as bait at this point, but there is no danger of their being hurt. We want to get word out that they will be seeing a show at the Golden Nugget tonight. We will be there in full force, although not visible to Manny or his men. He is in town now and probably eating or drinking with some of his men as we speak. We're checking the hotels and we should have word very soon on his whereabouts.

I'll see you at the fire scene. I'm five minutes out."

Chapter Twenty-Three

"This is Manny. Is this Benny?"

"Yeah, how's it going?"

"I'm in town for a job and I need some support. You got five good shooters?"

"I can do that for you. Where will you be in a half hour?" asked Benjamin.

"Come to my hotel. I'm at the Wynn. I'll have some food and drinks brought up and we can discuss what I need done tonight. Ruiz and his partner are at a motel near here. I'll get the location and we can meet them after we talk."

Manny was very pleased with himself now. He had people he trusted that could watch his back and help him eliminate the only people who could identify his men and possibly link him to their activities. He took a quick shower and called the front desk for room service.

"Ruiz, where are you guys?" Manny snapped into the phone.

"We're not feeling very well. We ate some bad shrimp earlier. When do you need us?"

"I'll call in a couple of hours," Manny said. "Tell me where you are."

Ruiz gave him the address and hung up the phone.

His partner yelled from the bathroom, "I think I am going to die."

"You better hope so because if Manny finds us sick there won't be enough of us left to bury."

"We should have stopped for a meal. Those shrimp didn't taste as good as they did a couple of days ago," Huey yelled from the bathroom.

"Let's get this place looking better, and smelling better," Ruiz said.

"I think I'm dying in here."

"It smells like it!" Ruiz shouted.

Chapter Twenty-Four

The fire had destroyed hundreds of acres of forest, as forest was described in Las Vegas, and the air was filled with particles that burned the eyes and nasal passages of those trying to determine what had happened. So many little Joshua trees had gone up in smoke and cactus melted down into pools of green slime.

"They have found the remains of two men according the fire marshal," Shawn said when he saw us.

"There was one body in the outhouse and one in what could have been Boo's trailer. We have the skull, which will give us dental record identification, a ring and, believe it or not, a wallet, which probably makes the dental search unnecessary. The body in the outhouse is in considerably better condition than the burnt remains in the trailer. A cursory exam suggests that smoke inhalation did him in. He was probably too afraid to come out or taken by surprise and not able to get out. It would have been a less traumatic death than the poor schmuck in the trailer who got fried," Shawn said.

"Mr. O'Reilly, I have the identification from the wallet of the man in the trailer. I'll run it through the computer and we should be able to locate some next of kin in short order," said one of the detectives collecting data at the scene.

"Look at this," Shawn said to Ricky, who was looking at the debris around the trailer.

"I knew I had heard that name before and I think I can put a story with this death. Joseph Gemmell is from San Diego. He was one of Manny's best importers. He would go to Panama, Central American and Mexico and select girls, buy their tickets to Northern Mexico around Nogales and Mexicali and have Manny's men take them from there to the States. Of course, when they were moved they were in vans or crates or trunks. They have even been successful getting them in on trains," Shawn said after reading the info on the license.

"This is or was Boo's husband," Ricky said shaking his head. "She won't take this well. That poor girl had a completely different picture of him. They fought a lot, but not over his business. He must have hated women a lot to do what he did. Luckily for Boo he did not send her to Manny."

Shawn was trying to puzzle out his thoughts. His mobile was ringing.

"Shawn O'Reilly?" The girl whispered into the phone.

"Yes," he said.

"Mr. Manny Rodriguez checked in two hours ago at the Wynn. He has called for room service, a rather large meal and a couple bottles of scotch. Two men have asked for him at reservations. I don't know if they went up. His phone line is red right now and has been for sometime. He did not ask for a check out date."

"Would this be Nancy?" asked Shawn.

"Yes sir it is," she said.

"I will leave you a card with the concierge, Nancy. Have a nice day." And he hung up.

"Well," he said to Ricky, Phillip and Juan. "It seems Manny has checked in at the Wynn and has a couple of visitors right now. Tonight holds promise of seeing these men in action. We need to get word out that we, with the ladies, will be at a show. I will have my best men around the theater as will Victor and Garcia. There could be no better protection in the states. I would have them guard me if need be."

"We will be there also," Ricky said. "We can be as inconspicuous as the next hit man."

"I will not mention this situation to Boo right now regarding Joseph," said Shawn. "I want her to look happy tonight not searching the crowd for her husband's killer."

"What time is the show?" Ricky asked.

"We will be in the hotel lobby at eight o'clock. That's just two hours from now. The show will start at 9:30 so the timing should be perfect," Shawn said. "I'll call Victor and Garcia. Then I'll call the Wynn and let our girl know how to let it leak to Manny that the girls will be at the show. She can let him know four new women just came to town and need the money to get home. She'll tell him they will be back about eleven-thirty after the nine-thirty show at the Nugget. They will be with some other clients while at the show, but alone when they return. I'll let her describe them to Manny and unless he is twice as stupid as I think he is, he will know those are the women he is looking for and be at the show not expecting our company," Shawn said.

Phillip asked Shawn for some bullet proof vests and something larger than the thirty-eight caliber revolvers they brought with them on this trip. Shawn sent them to the police station "game room" where they were to be given access to firearms of their choice.

It was getting closer to show time so Ricky, Phillip, and Juan each took a Glock 31 from the police armory and headed off to the hotel's designer clothing shop to buy new wardrobes helping to validate their new assumed identities, perhaps something with a Vegas high roller theme.

"This is on the expense account?" asked Juan. As Ricky nodded a yes, Juan went for the more expensive jacket.

"I would have bought this myself if you hadn't said yes," he smiled. "Some things you can only get in Vegas."

Juan selected a light gray rayon silk blend jacket and the lightest of gray slacks with some gray leather shoes and no socks. A silk carbon black shirt designed to be worn with an open collar was a perfect contrast.

Phillip ended up in a cream linen jacket with a dark tan shirt. He finished with a pink and tan tie, light honey color slacks and buckskin toned huaraches.

"You guys are worse than shopping with girls!" said Ricky.

Ricky, however, took the longest time getting just the right fit from the viscose blazer in azure blue. He wore it with tan slacks, tan sandals, and no socks. He too left the collar of a striped tan and azure blue shirt opened showing soft black hair peeking out the top.

They got the nod of approval from the shop owner and out they went, to the theatre. They noticed women looking at them as they passed in the large corridors and knew they were looking good. There were only three women they hoped to impress tonight.

Chapter Twenty-Five

"Mr. Rodriguez? There are four women who came to town today who were looking for some gentlemen tonight. I think they were from San Diego and in hopes of getting some easy cash. I'm told they are very pretty and they have arranged to meet their clients tonight at the Golden Nugget theatre, which should get them back to the hotel by eleven-thirty. I thought you may be pleased to know this. Would that work for you Mr. Rodriguez?"

"That'll work fine. Thank you. Do you have their phone number?" Manny questioned her.

"We are not allowed to give that information out sir. We can accept or decline appointments for their time. That is all."

"Accept it then. I might see them at the show. I'll know a new face in the crowd. I'll leave money at the front desk in an envelope."

"Thank you sir," Nancy said, and then dialed Shawn.

"Mr. O'Reilly?" asked Nancy.

"Yes, this is Shawn."

"Mr. Rodriquez has made an appointment to have the girls at his room at eleven-thirty. He also said he might check them out at the show, just in case he didn't like their looks."

"Thank you Nancy. Again, we are in your debt."

Chapter Twenty-Six

"I am too sick to come out of this bathroom," said Ruiz's partner.

"Damn it!" said Ruiz. "I need that toilet right now! Don't make me come in there. It will be a real shit fight."

"How much longer before he gets here?"

"Twenty minutes," Ruiz said.

"Call him and tell him we'll meet him outside, that we had a plumbing problem or some shittin thing," Huey said in a strained voice. "Get it, some shitten thing?" He laughed out loud.

"That's the first good idea you've had since I've known you. I'll call him. Now get the hell out of there or I'll shoot you."

"Manny, this is Ruiz. We've had a plumbing problem in the motel room. We'll meet you in front by the red SUV. What are you driving?"

"I don't have a fucking clue. Benny is picking me up. I will see you two, that's for fucking sure. I will just look for a fire or a flood." Manny slammed the receiver down.

"Smart ass bastard," said Ruiz. "He better pay us something for this God damn trip. Killing those women would not be payment enough."

Ruiz ran for the bathroom almost knocking Huey off his feet.

"I need a shower," Huey said as Ruiz ran passed.

"No time, use the cologne on the desk."

"I already used the air freshener from the bathroom."

Manny was on his way.

Chapter Twenty-Seven

Shawn was at the front door of the Nugget at seven-thirty. He had asked Garcia and Danni to bring some girls who could help provide some camouflage, some real attention getters, assuring them they would be in no danger. Shawn would never work a set up with anyone but himself as a target. Everyone who worked for him knew when Shawn was on a job he was front man and would risk himself over any of his people.

Shawn was feeling more comfortable with the arrival of Ricky, Phillip and Juan. He had a good feeling about their sincerity and skill. He knew they would not jeopardize the women they were after and that they would be good back-up when all hell broke loose.

Garcia and Victor tended to draw attention wherever they went. That was the strategy that they needed tonight. The more the crowd was looking at the beautiful people the less attention would be going to the police. Both men and women noticed them when they entered the lobby. Now, together with Sylvia, Mattie, Lucy, Boo and me by their side, we were quite a lovely sight. Single men moved in a little closer, which helped in Shawn's opinion, to protect the ladies even more.

It was at that moment Lucy spotted Juan, Ricky and Phillip on the far side of the lobby. I looked at her and followed her gaze directly to them. My God they looked good. We were warned not to acknowledge anyone so we looked away, not giving Manny or any of his sidekicks the opportunity to single out those who were there for our protection.

My heart was racing as I turned to Lucy, Boo and Mattie.

"My God," I said to them, with no expression on my face. "Are those the most beautiful men you have ever seen?" I knew this was Cowboy, but how did he get from my dream to Las Vegas!

"They are three of the most beautiful. Garcia, his men, Victor, Danni or Josh would not be thrown out of my bed!" Boo said with no expression on her face.

It was getting close to eight o'clock and pre sold tickets were being picked up and new tickets purchased. The lobby was full.

Ricky saw the women and said to Juan and Phillip, "Don't look now, but I think I'm in love." They immediately turned to stare in the direction Ricky was carefully studying.

"They changed clothes!" Phillip said showing approval on his face. "I can't wait for this to be over and those ladies under my protection. And I do mean under."

"No longing looks or identifying now. We need to find that asshole Manny and the men he has with him. We only have Shawn's description of him and that is pretty generic for the crowd here."

Shawn went to the concierge desk and returned giving them a heads up sign.

Over the loudspeaker we heard, *"VIP seating tickets now available for rows one thru four at line five only. Thank you."*

Shawn and Ricky then went to the area where the VIP tickets were being sold. Phillip and Juan stood at the far end of the counter where they could see all from the mirrored reflection of the lobby.

There were eleven men in the lobby waiting for Manny to move. Now where was Manny?

Chapter Twenty Eight

After picking up Ruiz and his partner in the parking lot at the motel, Manny, Benny and four of Benny's men went to the parking garage at the Nugget. They were in a Hummer, black with limo tint windows. The two in the extreme back were loading the guns they would take into the show. They had to be able to put them in their jackets, so no rifles, mostly forty-five caliber pistols.

"What about drink money?" Ruiz finally asked.

Manny ignored him. Then he said, "I gave that to the car bomber! Mendez was Benny's boy."

They parked and walked into the south side of the hotel lobby.

Manny handed two general seating show tickets to Ruiz and his partner, which he had picked up from the Wynn concierge. They were both still sick and really needed a restroom. Neither would speak, Manny was not in good humor. He mocked the way they looked and said he was sorry he knew them. He told them not to talk to him unless he spoke first. Realizing that may prevent them from telling him when they saw the women he said, "Unless you see the god damn women."

Manny and Benny pushed their way to the front of the first line they came to. "Give us two seats up close," he spewed at the cashier.

"Those are sold in line five only at this time sir. Those would be the VIP tickets for rows one thru four."

"Sell me the damn tickets here," Manny said. "You've got the same machine."

"I am sorry sir, but you will have to go to line five. You will get a free beverage ticket for your inconvenience sir."

"Jesus Christ," Manny said and moved down the counter to the line numbered five.

Shawn saw him and told Ricky. They saw the other man with him, who Shawn knew as Benjamin. Benjamin had a pawn shop on the east side that sold mostly stolen goods. Shawn and Ricky knew there were others, but they needed to identify them before moving in.

Chapter Twenty-Nine

Ruiz and his partner were heading for the men's room first before going to their seats in the back center section of the theatre.

"I have to stop here or I'll crap my pants," said his partner.

"Manny's not gonna like us late to that show. He's thinking we are backing him up," said Ruiz.

"He's not gonna like us shittin our pants and then being with him either," said the partner.

"How long can this take, five minutes?" Huey said. "There can't be much food left inside me!"

"Hurry your ass up, I'll watch the hall," Ruiz said. He went to the bathroom door and glanced down the hall toward the ticket counter.

His partner had just bolted himself in the stall when Ruiz saw the tallest of the bitches with another whore he didn't know coming down the hall. Christ, he thought, should I take em now? Just behind them was a man that was really dressed up who yelled something at the women and they stopped.

Ricky said to Boo as she stopped and turned, "Thank God you are alright. You shouldn't wander off without someone by your side and he hugged her tight."

Ruiz saw this and knew he was a customer of those whores and he slipped back into the alcove of the men's room.

"Ricky, this is Sylvia. She is with Victor and his men. She lives with Victor's family."

"Very nice to meet you," Ricky said. "You two are too beautiful to be walking around by yourselves. Boo, we have your credit cards and purses, but no ID was in the wallets. I think those bastards wanted the addresses. Shawn is certain they will be here tonight and we're hoping he's right."

Just at that moment Boo looked over Ricky's shoulder and saw one of the men from the van looking out from the alcove. He was talking to someone over his shoulder. Ruiz yelled into the stalls, "I see one of those bitches with her customer right outside this room."

"That was one of the men from the van I just saw behind you Ricky, going into that restroom!" Boo said.

Ricky turned and saw no one, but turned to Boo and Sylvia and told them to get back to the lobby and let Danni or Shawn know that those men are here.

"I will wait until I see them come out and try to stop them before they get into the crowd. Anything you can tell me about his clothes?"

"He looks like a dirty troll in gnome clothes. His jacket is green," she said. "He is not quite six feet tall and is red skinned with black hair. Remember the three stooges? He looks like a big Moe."

"Great, thanks," Ricky laughed. "Now get safe. Where is Sissy?" He had to ask.

"She is with us. She is missing you as well," Boo smiled.

Boo and Silvia went straight to Danni and he went directly to Shawn. Both Danni and Shawn were in the hall immediately beside Ricky.

"No one has left that room yet," said Ricky. "There is not another door. They must be waiting. How long do they think we will stand here?"

"Let's not wait on them," said Shawn. "Be careful. They'll no doubt have guns and have them aimed on anyone opening that door."

They entered the alcove and Shawn kicked the door open. The air was permeated with an awful smell. Two of the stalls were closed and there were no feet showing.

"Could these men be this stupid?" Ricky said looking at Danni, who was standing outside one of the closed stalls. He put his foot up and kicked the door into the stall, right off the hinges and into Huey who was standing on the toilet.

"Christ, I think you broke my legs," he howled. "You son-of-a-bitch, Manny will kill you. Oh Christ, my legs," he wailed.

A gun went off in the next stall and a bullet went thru the door breaking the mirror on the opposite wall. Shawn fired into the stall two feet, four feet and six feet high.

There was a groan from the inside and Ruiz slid off the toilet onto the tile floor. There was a lot of blood coming from the man and no one was making a call to 911. Shawn put a wooden wedge on the entrance door so no one could enter.

"You are two of Manny's dummies!" Shawn said. "If you were his back up he's screwed. I hope he didn't pay you already. He wastes a lot of money on shit heads like you."

"We weren't all his back up." screamed Huey, still in pain. "He has six others and they will find you and kill you and those goddamn women."

"Shut up!" Ruiz said, loosing his voice and his consciousness.

Chapter Thirty

It was almost nine o'clock and the guests were being let into the theatre for seating.

Shawn was now keenly aware there were at least six others in the crowd with guns. He was afraid they would have little concern for the innocent bystanders in the theatre if they decided to start firing.

He passed this news to Garcia so he could alert his men on the number of Manny's men somewhere in the congested theatre.

Then Ricky warned Phillip and Juan to be on the lookout. Danni would let Victor and his people know that they had six others to contend with so to watch their backs.

"Two of them are down," Ricky said, "and if the others are as stupid as those two, they may come to us and ask permission before shooting."

Boo and Sylvia joined Lucy, Mattie and I and told us she saw one of the men that had been in the van.

"Ricky sent us back to join you so we would be out of harms way. We left before seeing what happened. He was one of those at the table in the restaurant," she said, a bit shaken. "What a horrible person. He sat next to the one we thought was left stuck to the table. He was the fat one on the opposite side that kept watching our boobs."

"I will watch for Ricky," I said, hoping in my heart they didn't have a problem with the guys in the bathroom.

"Shawn and Danni were there too," said Sylvia. "They probably did not have much of a chance once those three got into the restroom. Let's join Victor and go in to see where he would like us to sit."

"He is talking with the girl who sells the VIP seating," Lucy said. "I saw him go up to her right after Manny and his friend left the counter."

Victor saw Sylvia and the rest of us standing against the wall waiting for him and our instructions.

"Ladies, let's join the VIP's in the fourth row, center aisle seating," said Victor. "Manny and Benjamin are two rows ahead so we are directly behind them by two rows. The lady at the counter said she would leave those seats empty until some very tall people came in and she would fill them that way if possible."

Victor would start the row, then Sylvia, Boo, and Mattie on the left aisle side of the center row in that order. Danni and I would be in the same row on the extreme right end on the aisle.

Putting Sylvia and Boo together gave them time to talk. They found comfort in one another. Sylvia seemed to have Boo's interests and cultural background in common. She knew Boo would be upset after learning of Joe's death and she felt a need to be close to her and protect her from any other possible consequences relating to Joe. Sylvia had suffered more than her fair share of pain prior to her current life with Victor. She had tried and tried to find work at a hotel on the strip as a dancer, but kept being offered prostitution jobs by none other than Manny. She managed to avoid confrontations with him for several months, realizing that there really was no one likely to help her or protect her from people like Manny. One night after she left a casino Manny had two men jump her and beat her unconscious. Very bloodied, she was found lying in a garbage strewn alley by a wino dumpster diver who took pity on her situation and called 911. It took over thirty minutes for 911 to respond and for the EMTs to get an IV running. With Sylvia's condition stabilized the ambulance rushed her to Las Vegas Mercy Hospital to undergo emergency facial reconstruction surgery. Victor was at the hospital that night also, finishing a heartbreaking visit with his wife who was dying of cancer. As he was leaving he passed Sylvia's bloody gurney being wheeled into the Emergency Room. Victor turned, asking the nurse in charge what had happened to her. The nurse replied that she was just a whore that they would have to sew up and send back on the street, rolling her eyes as she smiled at Victor. Probably no insurance she told him. Victor, who had two sons, a beautiful wife he was losing, and a home large enough to care for many, went straight to the head of the cosmetic surgery department and instructed him to give Sylvia the finest care available and to fire the duty nurse at the front desk.

The hospital administrator was initially perplexed by Victor's forwardness, but he was well aware of the amount donated to the hospital by Victor each year. The request really required minimal effort on his part and he was already unhappy with the duty nurse's performance, so he was happy to comply with the requests and let Victor think he had done him a solid favor.

After four weeks of recovery in the hospital Sylvia was strong enough to move in with Victor and his family. Although still weak herself she doted on Victor's wife and tried to ease the pain of what everyone knew were her final days. Sadly, and despite everyone's heartfelt efforts, his wife succumbed to the cancer only a month after Sylvia had moved in. Sylvia then found herself in the somewhat odd situation of being both a grieving friend and a surrogate mother to Victor's sons. Victor was desperate to keep his family intact after losing his beautiful wife and taking Sylvia in filled the void for him. Making room for another woman to live and work from his home was a joy for him, helped preserve his sanity and kept him from falling into a deep depression after the loss of his soul mate and wife. Sylvia remembered this as if it were yesterday.

Victor continued with his seating plan. "Lucy will be with Juan as a couple, Ricky and Phillip next to them. Shawn will be covering from several rows back and our men are placed closest to the exit doors, in what we hope, are the darker areas. They could be sitting next to Manny's or Benjamin's people for all we know, but we will find out shortly. The drink tables in front of the seating are ideal for concealing a gun. We'll have drinks on the tables so we look like guests, but our faces are known in this city so we may encounter greetings from acquaintances. Be prepared to drop on command ladies," Victor said winking at Sylvia.

Manny was standing to fake a stretch and look around to the far corners of the room. That helped to determine where his protection was seated. He seemed pleased with most placements, but not on the back of the theatre where he told Ruiz and his partner to stay. He scratched his head and bent down to Benjamin speaking into his ear. Benjamin shrugged and Manny sat down. Benjamin felt those two were not very important. He thought that six men could easily eliminate four goddamn women and this whole rotten plan was overkill, but he owed Manny a lot of money for women and laborers so he went along with his plan. Benjamin needed Manny's laborers to haul stolen merchandise from stores across town and to unload vacant houses while the owners vacationed. He never paid them what he promised and if they left, he just got more. He used the women as entertainment in card games, and actually as stakes. When he ran out of money, he bet the illegals. He lost a lot of them, but he knew he had good credit with Manny and could get more.

Where were those fucking guys Manny thought? They were the only ones who actually knew the faces of the women he wanted to kill. Without the women's testimony nothing could be proven on the van with the aliens. Anyone could have operated that van, not just his men. The charges would be dropped against him without those women to testify. Now that their car was gone and their trailer was gone, they would not be leaving town tonight.

What had happened to Joe? Manny needed to find out. Who killed him and put him in that trailer? Could that Goddamn Ruiz have killed him and told him a story about just finding him there?

He'd get that out of Ruiz after this bullshit was over. He needed Joe. Joe had a lot of his money. Joe knew all of the transporters, the cities of origin, and the men trusted him. Manny never experienced the bullshit he did with his other importers from Joe. Joe had records from fifteen years back. He always gave the originals to Manny, but he was to keep exact copies in the event something happened to

Manny. The business would be divided between Joe and Manny's son, Mio, if Manny was killed or put in prison. Mio wasn't old enough yet to manage the business but now, without Joe, Manny would have to introduce Mio to parts of the business he felt he could handle.

Maybe he could find out who Joe was married to a few years back. He never asked Joe about his wife. Joe would never discuss her and he never brought her to any affairs in San Diego or Las Vegas. She was to know nothing about his business. They must have been very much in love Manny thought. Manny would have to find her when this was over. He would take her flowers and pretend to be mourning her loss until he won her trust. Then he would find and steal the information from her home. She would have Joe's computer and probably without knowing, the records of bank accounts. He had to have that information.

He would leave for San Diego after this was over. He had Joe's home address.

Chapter Thirty-One

Raphael was getting ready to run a couple of the ladies to an engagement when the phone rang.

"Raphael?" Garcia asked.

"Yes, Mr. Garcia."

"Are you busy right now?"

"I was on my way to an appointment for two members. Can I help you?" Raphael asked.

"When you have finished driving them to their appointments, come by the Golden Nugget. Shawn has a couple of gentlemen that need to go to our east side house. They will have friends joining them later. I cannot tell you how many others right now but Shawn does not want them at the police station."

"I can do that. South side?" asked Raphael.

"Come into the men's restroom on the south side. There is tape closing the area off and two uniformed policemen inside with our guests. They will escort them to your car and ride to the location with you. They will not stay however. Victor has men there now waiting to help with questioning," Garcia said.

"Got it," Raphael said.

"Thanks."

One of Manny's men on the far right side of the theatre raised his hand for a brief wave to Manny or Benjamin. Garcia saw him. So that was the location of one. He was on Danni's side of the theatre and Danni saw the wave and knew what he had to do next.

Danni stood to let me out with the pretense of going to the restroom. The exit sign was right above the location of Manny's person. As we walked by the row Danni saw one of his own men in the same row, closer to the wall than Manny's guy. Danni's associate stood to leave the row and crowded in front of Manny's gunman at the same time Danni passed the end of the row.

The guy gave a groan as Danni's associate stepped hard on his shoe.

"Christ, watch where you're going asshole," he said.

"Do you want to take it outside?" Danni's associate said.

The man stood and, shoving his leg into Danni's associate, got up to follow him out the door. Manny must have seen this because he stood and looked in that direction.

"He's just going to piss," said Benjamin. "You're too jumpy. We'll get these bitches in no time. Take a squint and see if any of the men appear to be in the company of escorts. They probably look overdressed and out of place in this motley crowd. Didn't that Sunny come with us tonight? He was in the back of the van. He must have seen what they looked like. I understood he's the one that pissed on their car."

"Who told you that?" Manny growled.

"Ruiz told one of my guys. Sunny bragged about it in the back seat."

"Where the hell is he now?" Manny asked.

"He's over there with Buzz. Take a walk over to him and have him look around and come back to us if he sees them."

Manny got out of his seat cutting in front of every one in the front row, stopping at the area where Sunny and the van operator, Buzz, were talking.

"Were you in the back of the van pissing on the cars behind you?" Manny asked.

"Just one car sir," he said.

"Did you get a look at the women in that car behind you?"

"Yeah, I saw them go in the coffee shop this morning when I waited for Geno to bring the coffee back to the cab. He was really pissed at them for some reason. He was really pissed all day. Seemed he wanted to kill someone real bad. We were staying away from him. He said no one trusted him enough to give him more responsibility and said he could do what any importer could do, only better. He said he would get noticed someday. Then he did, at that restaurant when that lady stuck his hand to the table. Yep, that got him noticed. They were pretty nice, them women, I mean."

"Why aren't you with Ruiz and that Huey character?" Manny asked.

"I have family in Las Vegas, sir. I like to see them when I am here," Sunny said.

"Did you see Joe Gemmell that day? He would have been at the point where you loaded the van. Did you see him? He would have been following the van in a new Chrysler," Manny questioned him.

"No sir, but I wasn't there until it was loaded and they picked me up at the corner. Geno could have seen him I guess. He was pissed already when I got in. There were too many people for the cab he kept saying."

"Go see if you recognize anyone," Manny snapped. "Come over to where Benny and I are sitting, he pointed, and tell me where they are if you see them, any one of them." Manny followed the first row railing back to his seat.

Sunny began walking up the aisle on the farthest side of the theatre. He walked down the aisles, east to west, starting in the back. Ricky and Juan saw him canvassing the crowd and asked Lucy to pretend to pick something up when he got a little closer.

Sunny was just steps away from their table and Lucy put her head down to fix a strap on her shoe. He walked on by still looking at faces in the crowd.

Almost to Manny, he saw Boo and Mattie just two rows behind sitting with another woman and a big black man. He knew that man. His name was Victor and he had girls in the Freemont area. Getting to Manny's row he whispered to him over Benjamin.

Manny started to turn, but then thought better of it and stayed perfectly still. His hand went into his pocket and he pulled a cell phone out and pushed in a number. There was a ringing sound several rows back from where Garcia was sitting. Not far from Shawn.

Phones were to be turned off in the theatre and there was an attendant immediately beside Manny's person asking him to surrender his phone. Upon the request of Shawn, the man was escorted from the theatre. Three down, five to go.

Out of the theatre, into the lobby, the man was cuffed and taken outside to a van waiting curbside to go to the eastside house. Raphael had already taken the first two.

The show would be starting in fifteen minutes.

Danni and I were still in the lobby on the pretense of going to the restroom and getting ready to return to the theatre. Danni's associate, who was also his cousin, and Manny's gunman had been pushing on one another since entering the lobby, cursing loudly at each other causing passer-bys to look in their direction. Danni had pushed the large man against the wall taking his gun from his belt. He felt his leg and found a rather ugly knife that hadn't been cleaned from previous work.

"What did you plan on doing with this, asshole?" Danni asked in low voice.

"If I didn't like the show I would have thrown it at a performer," he snapped back. "You don't have anything on me, you bastard. You aren't the police. You better get your hands off me before someone sees you. I have friends here. They'll be looking for me real soon."

Danni kneed him in the stomach. His associate taped his mouth and put him in the electrical room adjacent to the exit door.

Four down, four to go.

Manny was getting hot just sitting still, wanting to turn around and face the women and man behind him. He had to see these people and was just about to turn and start shooting when he noticed that his right hand man had not come back in yet. How long could the son of a bitch stay in the toilet? Five minutes more and then he would start firing. Leaning over to Benny he told him there were two of the women two rows back with another woman and black man Sunny thought he knew from Las Vegas. He hadn't turned yet, but Sunny told him they were there.

Mendez, who had earlier fire bombed the car in the garage was one of Manny's men who was still at his location on the east exit. Sunny was sent back to the rear door area so he could open fire on anyone he recognized running out the door. Manny was confident that he would see the other women from that view point.

Boo was talking to Sylvia about Joe and how the two of them had fought before she left. "I guess I thought he would always be with me and we would never part," Boo said, knowing his actual whereabouts in the trailer and glad they had parted. She would no longer have to wonder how she would get rid of his body thanks to some greedy bastard who wanted the trailer.

Victor had told Sylvia all about the wallet and the burned bodies and asked that she not mention it to Boo until this mess was cleared up. She no doubt would be sad and possibly cry Victor told Sylvia. Sylvia agreed to honor Victor's request and kept silent about the whole sordid affair.

That's when the gunshots started. Sylvia and Boo looked straight ahead to where Manny was standing firing like a madman. Benjamin stepped out onto the aisle firing at one of Shawn's gunman sitting behind Victor, Sylvia, Boo and Mattie. The three women leaned far to the side so the seats in front provided cover. Victor reached for Manny but got only his jacket sleeve as he pulled free. Ricky and Phillip were firing over Lucy's head, as she dropped to the floor for protection.

The people in the theatre, rather than run, seemed to all hit the floor screaming at once. One elderly couple, thinking it was part of the pre-show stayed upright watching all the commotion.

Juan, from the far end of the row, began firing at the east side of the theatre where a man stood at the exit sign firing at Ricky and Phillip.

Danni hustled into the theatre from the lobby with me close behind, and hurled the dirty knife he had wrestled off the thug in the lobby directly at Manny. More than a bit surprised at his accuracy

Danni's knife struck Manny in the leg, just an inch from his crotch, and he sank to the floor screaming in pain and bleeding profusely.

Benjamin's luck was no better as he tried to push his way to the east side of the theatre and he took a bullet in the back, falling down on the two unfortunate elderly folks who had been watching the show.

Sunny pushed through the exit doors of the theatre, planning to escape to the alley and the safety of the car. Outside of the theatre doors cigarette smoke filled the air, and there stood Raphael with a forty-five in his hand. He shot twice as Sunny raised his gun to fire on him and Sunny was down, possibly dead. Raphael was in a take no prisoner's mood. He had been hired by Garcia because of the countless times he had the wisdom to be at the right place at the right time and his intuition was paying off in spades tonight.

Shawn had the good sense to cover the east exit where the man firing on Ricky and Phillip pushed through to run toward the alley outside the Nugget. Shawn shouted to stop, but the man decided he was quicker than Shawn's bullet and hit the exit door to the alley, just as a bullet hit his ankle. He rolled on the pavement, still hoping he had at least a slim chance of getting out of the melee at the theater. But that wasn't going to happen.

Shawn's men in the alley sent two police dogs after him, grabbing his pants leg and dragging him down. Blood was leaking through his sock onto the pavement.

A drug deal taking place in the alley came to an abrupt halt and five to six men scattered as the gunfire and police dogs filled the area.

Victor turned to get Sylvia, Boo and Mattie to safety. Looking at the women he became dizzy and felt his heart slow as he saw Sylvia in her seat with blood on the front of her dress. He was enraged as he bent and lifted Sylvia to him. She was looking at him through closing brown eyes a half smile on her face.

"Please, my pretty one, hold on, for the love of Christ hold on Sylvia." He was dialing 911 on his phone as he held her tight with one strong arm, but there was no need. The ambulance had come minutes before when someone from the casino had heard the shots and called 911. The paramedics entered and Victor called to them for immediate attention to Sylvia. They stabilized Sylvia, transferred her to a stretcher and loaded her in the ambulance. The EMT driver commented that their patient looked vaguely familiar. Boo climbed in the back to comfort Sylvia, the siren and emergency lights were flicked on and once again after a multi year hiatus Sylvia found herself on route to triage and treatment at Las Vegas Mercy Hospital.

Victor appeared to be almost twice his normal size as he rushed over to Manny, who was lying on the floor, the knife protruding from his thigh. With the utmost ease he lifted Manny up off the floor in a single swoop and threw him like a ragdoll at the stage.

"If that woman dies, you will be alive for a very long time with me. You will wish for death every second. You will pray to whatever God you believe in that you were dead," threatened Victor. "You are not going to a hospital you son of a bitch. You are going to join the rest of your fucking pin heads. I won't let you die you whiney ass little woman killer," Victor screamed to his face.

Danni, Josh, Shawn and Garcia, had never seen Victor as angry as he was at that moment. This was so far beyond anger that even they were afraid to speak to him.

Finally Garcia said in a gentle voice, "Come with me my friend, we'll go to the hospital and stay with Sylvia. These fools will be taken to the eastside safe house to join their friends. Raphael will escort them along with two of Shawn's men. Shawn's men won't stay at the eastside house; they'll just provide the delivery."

"I don't want Shawn's men there, just our men. The police should not be part of what will happen there," Victor said reinforcing what Garcia had just told him.

"Of course," said Garcia. He gave Danni clear instructions on what should happen next and then headed off to the hospital with Victor.

Ricky had a flesh wound on his right shoulder. I was immediately tempted to cradle him and kiss away his pain, but he was going to a medic to have it bandaged.

"Ricky," I said.

"Hi, I could only hope that you would stay out in the lobby and not walk back in to that gunfire. Did Danni get the guy that followed you out?"

"Oh yes Ricky. Danni and one of his men put him in a closet and then they sent him to a location somewhere with the others that were with that awful Manny."

"I'll see you a little later kiddo," he said in his best Bogart voice and turned for the medic.

Over the loudspeaker they were announcing a cancellation of the nine-thirty show. Dinner and free drinks would be provided for all guests at any of the hotel restaurants. Ticket prices would be refunded or honored at another show and time.

Shawn was re-directing the police officers scattered around the theater to new strategic locations around Las Vegas. Cameras were shooting pictures of the dead and a flock of news media vultures were gathering outside the theatre doors. A full moon was forecast that night which always seemed to produce some of the oddest and most unpredictable behavior in the month's activity log. Phillip was holding Mattie, trying to comfort her, and stroking her hair. Juan was helping Lucy crawl out from her hiding place under the table and smiling at her disheveled attire.

"I have gum on my knee," Lucy said followed by, "ick!"

Danni, Ricky, Juan and Phillip would be heading out to join the men at the eastside house.

Chapter Thirty-Two

Victor burst into the hospital lobby and headed directly to the Admissions counter. "Where will I find Sylvia Porter, a gunshot victim? She just came in by ambulance?"

Deciding to forego the "Are you family?" question, the intimidated counter nurse quickly gave him instructions on where to find Ms. Porter's room.

Victor, taking long strides, with his friend Garcia at his side, came to Sylvia's room and gently opened the door. She was not there and his heart skipped a few beats as a cold sweat covered his body.

"Sir," said the attending nurse, "she is still in the operating room. They're removing a bullet from her shoulder and then she will probably be in the Recovery Room for another hour. Would you like to have coffee?"

Victor felt like fainting, but steadied himself against the corridor wall trying to regain his composure and slow his heart rate. He caught a glimpse of Boo sitting on a bench down the hall by the operating room and went to sit by her side. He reached out and took Boo's hand and held it to his mouth, gently kissing it as his tears wet her skin.

She looked at him and saw all of the love he had for Sylvia in those big brown eyes. In his weakness he was beautiful, like a little boy who had lost a puppy.

"She'll be fine Victor," Boo said. "I know she will. She's very strong and certainly doesn't want to leave you behind. I would like to stay with her for a while here in Las Vegas while she mends. I hope that will be alright with you? I have little to go home to, just more arguments."

If only she knew, thought Victor. Her husband was dead, but he could not tell her right now. Not while she was caring for Sylvia and depending on him to bring Sylvia out of this place back their home.

"I welcome you to stay as long as you wish. Sylvia so enjoys your company and she will need you more than you can imagine. She is so used to being in charge of everything in our home so your presence will be a delightful gift for her," said Victor.

He looked at her blushing cheeks and wondered how she could have been with Joe Gemmell. He was such a low life. How she ever could have found him to be a loving husband was something Victor could not imagine.

Garcia squeezed his shoulder and told him he would go the eastside house and see that all was in order. He would have Raphael come from the house and wait for him downstairs.

"Thank you my friend. I thought I would be a better protector. My heart is filled with shame. This woman who has given me every moment of happiness since my wife's death may leave me without ever knowing what's in my heart," Victor whispered.

"Please, Victor, this was not a fault of yours. Far too many bullets started flying all at one time. Who would think that stupid son-of-a-bitch would turn and start shooting, like a mad man," said Garcia.

For the next hour Boo held Victor's hand until a vey kind petite nurse came and said Sylvia was in her room. She was out of any danger, but would have to be at the hospital a while longer for monitoring. The bullet was removed and there was no damage to internal organs, but she was suffering from shock and blood loss and would be quite sore for a several weeks. Then she told Victor that Sylvia would need to rest and to stay off her feet.

Victor stood and handed the nurse a large wad of twenty dollar bills. "Please take this money to cover anything that she needs. And please don't leave her alone or unsupervised. She's my princess and she deserves to be treated like one."

Tears formed in the nurse's eyes as she gently embraced Victor, smiled softly, and said, "I thought only God could love like that."

Victor looked in on Sylvia as she slept. Her long lashes lay across her cheeks and her flawless skin looked like the finest china. He held his breath afraid of waking her and brushed a kiss on her forehead. She still smelled of Shalimar. He remembered the first time he brought her that fragrance and she had not quit wearing it since. She cared so much for everyone and took so little for herself. He wanted to protect her from the moment he saw her in the hospital so many years ago. This was the first time he felt he let her down.

"You go now," said Boo. "I will wait and the minute she starts to wake I will phone you."

"Thank you Boo. Thank you with all my heart."

"Boo?"

"Yes?"

"If anyone comes in this room that you even remotely suspect as a person who should not be here, call me please."

"Oh I will, absolutely," she said. "I won't let anything happen to her. I don't always behave like a lady, especially if there is a dinner knife around!"

Victor smiled and turned to leave.

If Joe wasn't dead, he would have killed him for certain after treating Boo like he did.

Chapter Thirty-Three

Boo was talking to Sylvia as she slept.

"You are truly blessed my dear Sylvia. Victor is so in love with you and so worried about you. I have never seen such a powerful love. Let's get you well and home so he may rest. I wish I could tell you about Joe, Sylvia. He was such a mean person and so hateful. I feel so badly about our last fight and hope I will not have to pay for what I did for the rest of my life. He did fall, but I pushed him. I had no plan when I left San Diego how I was going to get rid of Joe. I just knew I would. It seems like my prayer was answered the moment I met my new friends and my trailer was taken. Perhaps with others he was a decent person, but with me he was cold and distant," she whispered as her head lay still on Sylvia's bed.

Boo laid her head there beside Sylvia and slept until she felt the movement of the sheets.

"Boo, is that you?" Sylvia whispered.

"Yes my dear friend," she said.

"I am so thirsty. Is there something here for me to drink with a straw?"

"There is. Here is some ice water. I must call Victor. He has been in hell since this happened."

"The poor man," Sylvia said. "He tries so hard to make everything perfect. He probably considers himself a total failure with this situation. I must talk to him and let him know I am fine and will be home as soon as possible." Her voice was so small, but Boo dialed Victor and gave Sylvia the phone when he answered.

"Hello," Sylvia said in the biggest parched voice she could find. "Have you had a decent meal yet? As I recall we didn't get any dinner after the theatre."

She thought she heard tears splashing on the phone as he tried to speak. Finally after some deep breaths the voice she loved so spoke to her.

"I won't eat until you can join me. I won't have a bite until you are home with me," Victor said, swallowing hard.

"Now, now, I will have good food here I am certain, so perhaps you can join me and share my plate?" Sylvia questioned.

"I am almost there. Don't start without me. We need to say a prayer," Victor whispered.

"May I talk to Boo, my dear?" Victor asked.

"Absolutely. I am waiting for you. Boo, Victor would like a word with you." Sylvia handed her the phone.

"She doing well and looks quite healthy considering what she's been through. She looks as if she had a spa treatment not surgery. She is extremely anxious to have you with her right now. Will you be long? I will tell her."

Boo hung up and went to get a brush to smooth Sylvia's hair. She fluffed her pillow and washed her face with a warm cloth. She put a dab of gloss on her lips and asked the nurse to bring her anything pink from the gift shop.

The nurse came back with a little chenille cape in bubblegum pink. It opened in the back and was meant for hospital wear. She found some white brushed cotton pants with an elastic waist, but thought better about putting them on Sylvia. "The doctor will be all over me if I disrupt her tubes ma'am," the nurse told Boo.

"That's ok," said Boo. "The top will be perfect and thank you. We will use the pants to go home in."

Boo helped the nurse replace the green top with the new pink top. Sylvia looked like Victor's queen, not just a princess, ready to receive court.

Chapter Thirty-Four

Victor was at the eastside house when Boo called. He was in the living room with Ruiz and his partner, Huey. Ruiz needed a doctor as much as Manny, but he did not care. The stench of these two was putrid. He wanted to know what happened to Joe Gemmell. He would not settle for a half ass answer from these two.

"Who killed Joe?" He asked.

"I don't know," Ruiz squealed. "He was dead when we found him in the trailer. He stunk. It could have been Geno. He got away from those police in Victorville. He could have been following us and run into Joe. We don't know, don't you understand. He could have put him in the trailer where we stole it from those women. That's Joe's job you know, keeping track of the haul and the time it gets to Vegas. Maybe he just decided to follow us and ran into Geno."

"Geno was real mad," said the partner, Huey. Both of Huey's knees were broken and swollen tight under his pants. "He was pissin all day about one thing or another. We wouldn't have been bad to those women if he hadn't wanted us to. He coulda killed Joe. He hated people in authority and he didn't like Joe cause Joe was short and mean and when the girls arrived down there Joe was the boss of Geno. Then Geno hated Manny because he didn't trust him enough with money or the papers. He always called Joe the short shit that slept with Manny. But the police took the van and there was no way

Joe could have been in with them. He had to be following us and maybe ran into Geno hitching for a ride."

Garcia and Victor wanted to kill them, but it was Manny who must die. These clowns were nothing without Manny. Someone would replace Manny for sure, but not for years. He was the worst kind of importer. He had absolutely no conscience. He could look at you and not see a thing. No life with a heart had meaning to him. He saw no beauty in women or family. He had been instrumental in so many men and women's deaths in Las Vegas alone. The police once took some of his real estate because of meth labs reported in his houses. He never cared. The house titles were buried in pseudo company names, not his. He ran dog fights outside the city but always managed to be long gone by the time police arrived. He was garbage and should be treated as such.

Victor told his men he had to go see Sylvia and not to give water, food, cigarettes or medical aid to the men in custody. Suffering was paramount for these men. He headed for the hospital with only the thought of Sylvia on his mind.

Ricky, Phillip, and Juan were in a large wood paneled room at the eastside house. They felt very much the same as Victor. Danni had told them Victor was not a man who practiced or participated in violence and there had to be some pretty unusual circumstances to have him behave as he had earlier. Sylvia was that circumstance. His life revolved around Sylvia's happiness. If she was happy he was king. If she was hurt he was the executioner.

Manny was tied to a chair in front of massive granite faced fireplace. The fire was blazing although it was hotter than hell outside. The heat from the fire was unbearable from across the room, but from where they placed Manny it was hot enough to blister skin. Manny was squirming and sweating like a pig. His leg had stopped bleeding, but it was in plastic wrap to keep the floor clean. Swearing continuously and yelling at the top of his lungs seemed to bother no one. The plastic looked as if was melting on his leg.

"No one can hear you," Danni said. "Save your voice for the real pain." Leaving, he closed the door behind him as well as the door of the room that held the others.

Garcia's men had pulled up chairs at a table to have drinks and food in the kitchen. Ricky, Juan and Phillip moved to the air conditioned porch looking out at the desert, bringing sandwiches and Danni with them to enjoy a few moments of conversation.

"I don't know how we will ever repay you for taking the ladies and keeping them safe with you. We thought for certain the worse had happened and we would be finding their slain bodies somewhere in Las Vegas," Ricky said.

"It was our pleasure," Danni said. "They were a sight in those clothes. Josh and I knew they were not in customary attire when we saw them. They were so concerned about not seeing themselves in any mirror that it made us laugh. There are so many women trying to work the streets by themselves, but we know what they look and dress like. They don't last as a rule, because of men like Manny. Your ladies did not have that presence. It was pure enjoyment watching them arrive at our home and then have what appeared to be a good time!"

"I know little about their history," said Phillip, "but I'm hoping I can be part of their future."

The men smiled.

Chapter Thirty-Five

Mattie, Lucy and I were the luckiest women in the world that night. First of all because we were not shot at the Nugget and second because Ricky had given us the key to their hotel room where we went as soon as the limo came so we could see Baby.

I opened the door and there was Baby, sitting up looking at the door as it opened. She ran towards us faster than I could imagine, knowing how sore her leg had been, and leapt up on Mattie. She licked her face and then turned to me and did the same. She needed to go for a walk, which was evident from the way she stood by the door so we put her new collar around her neck that we purchased from the Nugget gift shop and headed for the hall. It was almost eleven at night but the casino lights were so bright outside that it seemed more like noon. Where else but in Las Vegas could you buy a flashing dog collar.

Baby was healing beautifully and I resolved to keep her as my dog forever and ever. Mattie and Lucy would have visiting rights, but this dog was part of my soul.

The cell phone rang and it was Ricky just checking in.

"Hi," he said. "Are you girls alright?"

"We're fine and are going to walk Baby right now. You did a fine job caring her for the last couple of days. She has a lot of your personality traits I think. She's been licking my face a lot!"

"You three should be perfectly alright at the hotel for the night. There is no one left to bother you, but Victor said he would like you three to go to his home with his family. Do you have a preference of where you would like to spend this evening?"

"Let me check with Mattie and Lucy," I said. "It took three seconds but it's unanimous; we are going to Victor's. Do you think it would be alright to bring Baby?"

"I'm certain he would love that. I've heard there is ample room for everyone including Baby at his home. Sylvia may still be at the hospital, but Boo would love to see Baby when she gets to Victors. We will have a driver there in one hour. Victor said there are clothes for you at his home so you could wait to change until you get there," Ricky said. "I can't be there to help you, unfortunately, but I will see you soon."

"Since we have no clothes to change into here going there makes even more sense!" I said. I hung up and felt a new giddiness, different from the earlier lust, which I hadn't had for a long time.

Lucy was holding Baby's leash as we walked down the street from the hotel. I was humming to myself, full of potential future bliss. We were just turning the corner when we heard several loud gun shots very close overhead. They were so close they shattered the glass windows in the apartments above the street where we were walking. We all crouched on the sidewalk as a car stopped a few car lengths ahead. Baby was barking and wanting to chase the vehicle. It took all of Lucy's strength to hold her. We needed to be inside anywhere right now. Staying in plain sight on the street was much too risky. Whoever was shooting at us would have to find a place to pull the car over and reload. We had a few minutes to seek safety since the driver couldn't stop on the Strip with all the traffic. It would no doubt draw the undue attention of other drivers, pedestrians and possibly a nearby traffic cop.

I called Ricky on my phone and described our precarious situation to him as we ducked into the closest casino.

"Jesus Christ," he said. "Stay in the casino, we will be there in five minutes." On the way to the casino Ricky called Shawn. Shawn said he would have whoever was closest go there immediately.

Mattie, Lucy, and I with Baby dropped into a booth in the casino's café located just inside the main entry doors. The waitress came and asked if she could help and then saw Baby.

"I am sorry but there are no animals allowed in the casino café," she said, very apologetically.

"She's blind." I pointed to Lucy. "She has to have her guide dog at all times."

"Oh, I am sorry, I did not notice. That will be fine. Let me know when you're ready to order."

I rummaged through my purse and handed Lucy my big sunglasses and that seemed to convey a more realistic blind person look. We sat there shivering for what seemed like an hour, but it was closer to five minutes.

Then we saw, from the booth, that horrible large van driver from the Victorville restaurant. His hand had a filthy bandage and he looked extremely angry, probably more so because he had to park his car. He was disheveled and dirty, his eyes darting to every person hoping to find us and end his mission.

Behind him we saw Phillip and Juan crossing the street, apparently heading for the same door. They had never seen the driver and would not know he was right next to us. I wanted to catch their attention, but that would blow our cover and expose our presence to that disgusting man who wouldn't be happy until we were dead.

The waitress came back to the table and trying not to appear desperate or explain our predicament I begged to borrow the flower patterned turquoise scarf that adorned her neck.

"Well it's part of my uniform for the restaurant, but if it's urgent I guess you could," she said. "I actually own several and they are so popular that we sell them in the casino gift shop for twelve dollars, but that's closed until next week due to remodeling."

"Thank you so much, we will pay you gladly," said Mattie, handing the waitress a twenty dollar bill for her trouble.

The waitress took off her scarf and gave it to us. I tied it around Lucy's hair and with the oversized glasses and Baby leading the way we sent her on her blind scouting mission to meet up with Phillip and Juan.

She left the booth feeling the walls for support and guidance, playing her new assumed handicapped role with dramatic effect, as she slowly navigated over to Juan. Reaching him she pointed to us as only a blind person could do, using a head nod, and then to the man from the van.

"It's that man that Boo stabbed with the steak knife! I thought they had found him and were holding him?" Lucy said questioning Juan.

Juan looked at her, a slight shrug to his shoulders, and gently guided her straight ahead towards the women's restroom, advising her to keep going until she was safely inside the inner door and not to come out until she heard his voice.

I saw Ricky pushing through the buffet line on the back side of the restaurant with two other men who undoubtedly were police. They went to Phillip and Juan and together they followed the man to the back of the casino. They split up and went down parallel aisles gently nudging people to the sides of the walkways asking that they stay clear for a short time. I watched Ricky disappear into the crowd and wished I had touched him before he got away.

I never believed clothes made the man, but they do show them off a whole lot better and even with the hole in Ricky's jacket shoulder and a smudge of blood on his neck he looked good, Cowboy good.

Shawn saw us as he entered and asked that we go to the women's restroom and stay there until he came to the door. He said there was a door stop behind the door and to use it when we reached Lucy and were safe inside.

We stood in the restroom throwing water on our faces and giving handfuls to Baby. This had been quite the vacation. We had made a new friend in Boo, moved a dead body across state lines, avoided being murdered a couple of times, met some fabulous men, wore designer clothes and eaten extremely well. Besides the almost getting killed part, and maybe the dead body, it was what a vacation was all about. The biggest surprise of all was Baby. How many people get a gift like her I thought?

While in the bathroom, for about twenty long minutes, we recounted our adventure so far and prayed for a happy resolution of the current unfolding events. Suddenly we heard Shawn's voice at the door.

"We have the man called Geno and he won't be your problem any longer," said Shawn. "Actually, he will be no ones problem."

We opened the door and heard that Geno had been killed while holding a hostage. He was shot from behind, not the cowboy way, but that was the only way to safely neutralize him and not endanger the hostage.

"Thank God. I thought he was in custody?" I questioned with some apprehension about who else might be lurking around.

"Yes, so did I," Shawn said. "He now is in permanent custody, without the expense of going to court."

Ricky, Phillip and Juan were coming down the hall. I walked to Ricky and touched his shoulder. "Are you feeling better?" I asked.

"I am now," he said and drew me to him for a kiss on the forehead. I so loved the gathering and touching part of affection that men so often forget.

Baby jumped up on Ricky's side, panting softly, clearly wanting a pat. She got several pats on the head and I realized I was almost jealous. He really did love animals. My mother always told me if men aren't good to animals and their mother, don't get involved. I went by that all of my life.

Mattie, Phillip, Lucy and Juan walked ahead of us to the curb where there was a car to take us to Victors.

"See if you can stay out of trouble for a while," Ricky said as we were tucked into the limo.

We threw kisses and were on our way.

Chapter Thirty-Six

We asked the limo driver to stop at the hospital on the way to Victor's so we could visit with Sylvia and Boo. The lobby was packed with a lot of misfits and emergency visitors waiting for care. The front desk nurse asked if we were family which we of course said, "yes, sisters," and got her room number. After locating her room we went in and were amazed at how many flowers fit into a standard hospital room!

"Wow! This room smells better than any perfume on the market. Look at these roses," I said.

"And the lilies," Lucy said.

"You have so many people that love you Sylvia," I said.

She smiled and said, "I think if you read the cards they are mostly from Victor. One bouquet would have been sufficient, but he is a bit extravagant at times. The one over in the corner is from Garcia and his boys. It is a real pink dogwood tree in full bloom. I can't wait to plant that at home off the main dining area on the balcony. I think Victor felt it too grand when he came in and then sent me every flower arrangement made in Vegas!"

"Sylvia, you look wonderful. Are you feeling well?" Mattie asked.

"Oh yes. The doctor said he thought I could go home in the early morning if I had a nurse stay with me for a couple of days. Victor was very much in favor of the idea. He has several friends that have gone to nursing school while they enjoyed life with us and so he will be contacting one immediately and then I can go home. I'll need to rent a van for the flowers," she beamed.

"Boo, we have missed you. We are staying at Victors tonight so we can all be together," I said.

"I am so glad," said Boo. "In the excitement at the hotel I haven't followed up on Baby or the men or anything."

"Oh Baby is looking fabulous. She is healing and being pampered so much she doesn't know what to do with herself. She is waiting in the limo downstairs. The guys are at a house on the eastside where they are questioning some men that lived through the theatre episode and they will come to the house in the morning. I don't know about their schedule tomorrow, but they will share that when they come to Victors," I told her. I really didn't want to leave the floral arrangements or their sweet fragrance that filled the room.

"I am going to stay on with Sylvia for a while," said Boo. "I would like her to be completely healed before I head back."

"I'm not surprised," I said. "She will love that."

"Boo will have lots to do because I will need to be pampered for a few days," Sylvia said with a laugh in her voice.

Sylvia still had not told Boo that Joe had been found dead, burned in the trailer that was stolen from us. She promised Victor she would wait.

I asked Boo if there was something I should do at her home when we returned to San Diego.

"There should be no need to go over there," she said. "Whatever is going on, I don't think I want to know. I think everything will be fine. Joe probably left for good like he always said he would. I will call my brother and let him know the trailer was stolen and the car was bombed and I am staying here for an undetermined period. He won't be worried; he'll be relieved I am well."

The nurse came into the room and said there would be papers for Sylvia to sign and then we could take her home early tomorrow.

That news made us all smile.

"I will call Victor," said Boo. "He should know we will need that limo bright and early. He will be a very happy man."

After Boo's call to Victor we all piled into the limo and headed to the house. Sylvia needed to sleep before the morning trip home.

Chapter Thirty-Seven

"I swear Ruiz, if you are not telling me everything you know about Joe I will skin you while you're still alive," said Garcia, smoking a cigar with the smoke wafting into Ruiz eyes.

"I don't know anymore than what I've said. He was dead and we burned the trailer in the park. We didn't plan on settin that fire. The tumbleweed and the brush just caught on fire and then everything was on fire and we got the hell out of there. Manny told us to burn the evidence."

"Yeah," his partner said. "He said he was going to kill us if we didn't and then he said he was going to kill us when we did. He said the women could identify the van drivers and they had to be killed. He said he was going to make them suffer tonight after the show and then kill them. We were supposed to tell him what they looked like, but you ruined that for us and now you won't let us have a doctor or anything."

"Give them some water," said Garcia. Danni asked someone at the door to get water, but nothing else. They left Ruiz and his partner and went to Manny's room.

Manny was still tied in the chair in front of the fireplace. He was hot and sweat was pouring off his face. He was the color of red raspberries and covered with hundreds of little blisters.

"You cock sucker, you'll pay or this," Manny howled.

"I don't think so Manny. Who will you tell? Your men are dead or tied up somewhere. Your main man, Joe Gemmell, is dead and that leaves a pretty big area that is not being covered right now for illegals to be bought and sold," Garcia said.

"Where's that fucking cop Shawn? He will make you let me go. You've got no cause to hold me. You got nothing on me. Some gun fire in the hotel, big fucking deal!" screamed Manny.

"Well, Shawn had to go, too much business this weekend in the city and so it's just you and me and some out of town police who don't know what you are all about."

Ricky was in the room with Manny. He said to Manny, "I thought you died in the gunfire. I haven't seen you since. You don't exist to us."

"You son-of-a-bitch! You were with that pussy from the SUV. It's gonna feel good to have her!" Manny raved.

"You'll be looking up from hell at her," Ricky laughed.

"So Manny, do you have any thing you want to tell us about Joe's death. It seems you might have wanted him dead. He knows a shitload about you and your business," Garcia asked.

"He was like a son to me, you asshole," Manny said. "I'll find his wife when I'm out of here and she'll tell me what happened. She lives in San Diego and she'll know if someone came to their house before this happened. I'll get my shit from her."

He did not know that Boo was Joe's wife. How ironic. At Boo's home were the files on all of his clients, the money he had not gotten from Joe and past records that would be worth gold in the right hands.

"Let's leave him to keep warm for a while Ricky," Garcia said.

They left the room and Garcia went to the phone to call Victor.

"Victor, it's Garcia, can we get a small plane to the private airstrip in the morning, early?"

"Of course, do you need some assistance?" Victor asked.

"Got it covered. I'm going to show a few men an aerial view of the fire they started earlier."

"Six o'clock, with pilot, and Victor, how is Sylvia?"

"She is doing better than expected, Garcia. She will be home as early as I can get her out tomorrow morning and Boo will be staying with us during her recovery. The other three women will stay tonight so I feel confident we have all the loose ends tied up. We will let Sylvia tell Boo about Joe tomorrow."

"It sounds like you will have a houseful. I imagine the police from Victorville will be joining the ladies there tomorrow? By the way, all of Joe's records can be found at Boo's house according to a very hurting Manny."

"The more the merrier," said Victor. "We have a lot to celebrate. I will send Josh and Danni over to San Diego to pick up Joe's personal files if that is alright with Boo. I will ask Boo after Sylvia tells her about his death tomorrow. I think she should know what Joe was and why it is important to have those files. She has a good heart. I don't want anyone else having that information. She'll understand. That is a good reason for her to be here for a while. If someone finds out who Joe's wife is and they trash the house, she will not be in harms way."

"Did you hear the escaped driver named Geno tried to kill the three women in town tonight?

"No. Are the women alright at this time?" Victor asked.

"Yes, Shawn and the boys from Victorville were there in a heartbeat. Everyone is alright and Geno is no more," said Garcia.

"That's great news," Victor sighed, "A lot of action for twenty-four hours."

"Indeed," said Garcia.

Victor was beyond anxious waiting for Sylvia to come home. He made the call for a plane to be ready for departure from the private airfield on the north side of town at six a.m. before he made his plans for Sylvia's arrival home. He was relieved to have her coming back so soon and would never let anything like this happen again. It had taken this close call for him to realize what life would be like without Sylvia. It would be unbearable. He wanted to marry Sylvia and have her share not only his life but every asset he owned. If he died she would not be left with everything he wanted her to have unless they were married. Danni and Josh would be generous with

Sylvia, but he would be so much more generous. It made him smile to think of her as his wife.

It was eleven o'clock that night when Victor phoned his jeweler, probably waking him, and asked that he create a very special pink diamond ring that would symbolize his devotion to Sylvia. Pink was her favorite color and the ring was to have three stones, one multi-carat pink center stone bordered on either side by a large carat white diamond. The band was to be platinum, size six, which he knew from previous purchases and, just to up the ante for the jeweler, Victor was adamant that it be finished by the following morning.

The time remaining before Sylvia came home was getting shorter and Victor needed to call his caterers to prepare a fabulous breakfast for tomorrow morning, notify friends to come and have the girls from San Diego get comfortable for the night. This was the good part of life. He felt very blessed. His sons would be happy for him and he would once again have a complete family.

Chapter Thirty-Eight

The plane arrived at the airport at six a.m. sharp. Danni, Ricky, Phillip, Juan, Garcia and Victor's pilot were already there.

They left Manny tied in the straight back chair, just as he had arrived in the SUV that brought him to the plane. He was pissed. He had no sleep and was blistered on his right side from his proximity to the fireplace at the eastside house. Ruiz and his partner were cuffed to one another and the one remaining man, one of Benjamin's shooters, was tied to the both of them.

"Let's get them in the plane," Garcia shouted over the engine which was left running.

Up they were lifted, tossed in unceremoniously and everyone else took a seat in the Cessna Twin. The plane taxied onto the tarmac, received clearance, and shot up into the early morning sunrise which was casting red and orange spears over everything in sight.

"Thought we might take a closer look at the little fire you morons started yesterday. It burnt over 1000 acres, displacing all of those little animals," Garcia said.

"Who gives a shit?" said Manny.

"Well, you should Manny. I want you to have a good look at the destruction you caused. It seems that wherever you go, people or animals are mistreated. I want to help correct that."

"Kiss my ass," he said.

Ruiz shouted at Manny, "It was your fault we started that fire. You told us to burn that body up or we would notta been there."

"Shut your mouth you idiot! I should have killed you earlier!" snapped Manny.

"I think you are a fuck face," Huey said to Manny. "I haven't ever liked you and I don't think many people do. You're a cheap son of a bitch too."

Ruiz smiled at his partner.

The plane was climbing and one of Garcia's men threw two parachutes at Manny and Benjamin's man. He cut the ropes that held Manny's back to his chair, leaving his lap still tied to the chair seat. Then he untied Benjamin's man from Ruiz and Huey and gave him a chute to put on.

"Put those on," commanded Garcia.

"What about us?" asked Ruiz, rather sheepishly, hoping they would get chutes too.

"We'll see how these work first," Garcia said sarcastically. "Now take a look at all that charred wood down there. Look at those little helpless trees that might fall over at the slightest wind. All that damage just because you did not want to contend with some minor questioning from our local police. I don't know how your son will ever fill your shoes, Manny. With any luck perhaps he took after his mother, whoever that might be."

"Fuck you," Manny said.

The cockpit was ablaze in the glare of the morning sunrise as Garcia's men moved Manny and Benjamin's man to the Cessna's door.

"Well, let's give those chutes a try shall we? Oh yeah and Manny, did you know Joe's wife was the beautiful tall woman sitting behind you at the Nugget? I didn't think so." They put them over the men's shoulders and showed them where the pull cords were. Both were thrown out of the plane in midair over the charred acres below. The other man must have known the futility in screaming as not a sound was made.

Time was passing and no chutes were opening. The Cessna was tilted to show the men plummeting to the blackened earth below.

Ruiz and his partner could not see out of the door, but they heard Garcia saying to the others, "Those were not the good chutes I guess. Do we have others here for Ruiz and Huey?"

They were quiet and sweating and staring at their laps. They were waiting to be thrown from the plane with or without a chute that did or did not open.

"What do you think, men? Want to give flying a try?" Garcia asked.

"No sir," they said in one voice.

"Do you believe in God boys?" Garcia questioned.

"We do, sir. We were listening to his tapes when we were coming into the city. They were really good. We both liked em enough to buy some more," Huey said.

"Well, I'll tell you what. I am going to let Shawn have you when we land and he will help you decide what you want to do with the rest of your life. Who knows, maybe you could change vocation and become an asset to him and his force, maybe not. That will be up to you." Garcia closed the door of the plane and sat back down to talk to Ricky.

Ruiz looked at his partner, and said. "Fucking Awful, that's it. That's what the **A** stands for."

His partner smiled a little smile and said, "Jesus Hallelujah. That's what the **H** is for." They felt very blessed at this moment.

"I think they may be of assistance in identifying many of what remains of Manny's company. They are actually just too stupid to kill. They would do anything for a meal and cheap entertainment and Shawn can improve on what they were getting just by showing them a little compassion. Manny liked to crush people and make them squirm. I think Shawn would like to give it a try, anyway. Manny was a threat and would have caused some serious problems left alive. Sorry you had to witness that," Garcia said.

"The cost of keeping men like that in prison is a drain on the system. They were given the opportunity to use the chute. It was their decision not to as we saw it," Ricky said approvingly.

Shawn was waiting for the plane when it landed and quickly took custody of Ruiz and Huey his partner. They would become good informants Shawn hoped. Some fresh clothes and a little pay and they might enjoy their new jobs. They would live in Vegas, which actually would not be all that bad, and report to Shawn on events happening in town. Good work if you could get it. If it didn't work out they would be charged with the murder of Joe Gemmell and sent to prison. It should be an easy decision to make.

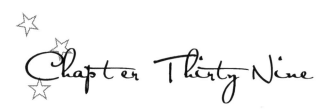

Chapter Thirty-Nine

"That's a full day's work," Ricky said to Garcia.

"I think we owe ourselves a nice breakfast and some fabulous company today," Garcia said.

"We'll head for our hotel and give you a call in a couple of hours. We have not been to Victors and I think it will take more than just our good looks and a badge at the front door to get in." Ricky laughed. "Maybe you could meet us in front of his place?"

"I'll call you at ten o'clock. That'll give you a couple of hours to make yourselves look better," Garcia laughed. "I'll be outside the entry gates with the code." He gave them the address.

Ricky, Phillip and Juan were anxious to see the girls, but first they needed to shave and shower, change clothes and maybe even get thirty minutes downtime. They grabbed a couple hours of sleep at the hotel last night before this morning's plane trip, but an hour now would make a world of difference later when they started the trip home.

Once in the hotel room, Ricky, Phillip and Juan found a sofa or a bed and landed on it for a short rest. Juan who landed closest to the phone called the front desk for a one hour wake up call.

"God this feels good," Ricky said. And they were asleep.

When the call came an hour later they all wanted to ignore it, but Juan picked it up and thanked the front desk.

It was time to get moving and they had less than an hour to clean up, change clothes and get to the address Garcia had given them. Hoping this day would be better than the last two days they finished dressing then checked out of the hotel and hit the road, looking forward to seeing the girls and checking out Victor's home. None wanted to leave the girls but this originally looked like a half day assignment when they got the call. They had some catch up at work to do when they got home. San Diego was not all that far from Ontario. It had been a long time since Ricky had been so drawn to a woman. Phillip had not dated for months and the Juan that Ricky and Phillip knew never engaged in conversation with any woman longer than a police appointment time. Now he talked continuously about Lucy when the men were together. They could only hope whatever happened in Las Vegas did not stay there.

With Sylvia home, Victor was a happy man. His face beamed when he looked at her. He requested that the nurse make a special lounge area in the living room for Sylvia so she could enjoy the day with all the others and be the center of attention. She was radiant he thought. She was dressed in a marine blue velveteen jacket with rhinestone buttons and matching slacks. She was having the manicurist work on her nails basking in the luxury of being home and waited on by everyone. Boo was sitting next to her.

"You look beautiful," Victor said to her as he watched her eyes twinkle. "I hope you will forgive me for the grave error I have made."

"What error would that be Victor? You were taking your favorite girls to the theatre," she said.

"I was not supposed to let them get injured," he said back, lovingly.

"Oh, Victor, that could have happened in Las Vegas under any circumstances. I am very glad for all of the loving attention I am getting from this mishap, but there really was no one at fault. Look at the lovely new friends I have made," she laughed.

"You deserve all this attention every day in your life Sylvia." He wanted to hold her hand, but her nails were still wet. "I will leave you women to do what it takes to get you ready for this day." Victor had a new lightness in his voice and in his step. Victor did look happy seeing Sylvia with her new friends. He turned adding, "Ricky, Phillip, Juan and Garcia will be here shortly for some brunch and a couple games of cards. This afternoon should be a wonderful time for everyone. There should be no one left who can dampen our spirits."

Boo smiled at Sylvia. Sylvia wanted to tell her about Joe. She asked for Victor to come back to her for just a moment and she asked him if that would be alright while they all were alone, not in the company of the men coming later. Sylvia thought it would be easier if Boo knew now and could digest it by the time company arrived. Sylvia knew she personally would not like to be told in a group of people about her husband's death, no matter how terrible the man had been to others.

Victor said that would be her decision, aware she knew Boo far better far than he did. He left the room and we were all looking through magazines and playing with Baby, waiting for Sylvia's nails to be completed.

"Boo," Sylvia said as she looked at us all scattered around the room, "could we all get together and have a little talk before the rest of the people come?"

We moved closer to Sylvia, hoping she was not feeling badly and needed to go to the hospital again.

"Boo, yesterday when they had found your trailer burned in the National Park the police had also found a body in the trailer that they were able to identify. After the remains had been examined, it was determined that the person in the trailer was one of Manny's managers, a man that obtained women from towns as far away as Panama for the sale of their services in the United States. He was not a good person and ruined many lives over the period of several years. The dead man reportedly kept extensive records of people, places and financial transactions tucked away in his home safe. Victor wants to go retrieve those files before anyone else can find them or find the man's wife and force her to reveal their hiding place."

We were all on the edge of our seats as Sylvia told this story. I was getting goose bumps knowing we were about to hear the sad tale of Joe's dead body. Who knew the scum sold women. I wanted to butt in and finish the story but I held my tongue.

"And this man, Boo, has been identified as Joseph Gemmell." Sylvia took a breath. "Victor was sick to his stomach after hearing the identification, knowing he was your husband and that Manny's men might have known that when they started harassing you on the way to Las Vegas. They can't be certain if Manny killed Joseph, but Shawn will close the case without much investigation. They were probably looking for a place to put Joe's body and the trailer was ideal. Victor fears for your life because of the records that he thinks may be at your home. Someone will know there are bank accounts, which of course are now all yours, but there is also a list of contacts and individuals that have used Manny's services. That critical information will be very important to Shawn as well as any competitors of Manny. I am sorry," Sylvia said sympathetically. "I have been rambling and not letting you have time to absorb this information. Come let me hold you for a time."

Boo walked over to Sylvia and laid her head on Sylvia's velveteen jacket. She said nothing right away, as Sylvia stroked her head, keeping her nails free from the hair.

We watched and held our breath until Boo spoke.

"How long was he in the trailer do you think?" Boo asked, weakly.

"They really don't know. They apparently killed him here and put his body in the trailer after they stole it from you. His remains were badly burned but his wallet had fallen from his pocket and was lying beside the trailer. The police were fortunately able to decipher Joe's name from the scorched driver's license. They'll confirm his identity through dental records. Shawn knew the name but did not put it together until Joe was found. No one was willing to acknowledge knowing where or when Joe was killed."

Boo didn't say anything but she stood up and slowly walked to the window facing the skyline of Las Vegas. She felt good inside, relieved and finally free of a heavy weight. She had done it and done it successfully. Her new friends knew and they wanted to remain in her life. Her body relaxed. Her prayers had finally been answered.

Perhaps she should have called the police, but at the time she felt it was better to just call her brother. She wanted to run to the shelter. She wasn't entirely certain the bastard was dead. But she did not know what he'd done to all those women. She did not know what his life had been all those years. A part of her wished she would have known and turned him in to the police, but now she realized they would have confiscated property and that would have been terrible. Fortunately she was not part of his life now, only part of his death.

She turned and said to her friends, "I cannot believe I was living with a man that could do such disgusting things to so many women and men, a man who could sell another human being and not display a moment's shame. All of those stories about not wanting to go the Las Vegas because of the sin and degradation and he was creating that very thing. He was participating in life's worst nightmare. I would rather he would have been selling drugs. I am ashamed for him and embarrassed to have been his wife."

"Boo," I said, "you knew nothing about the real Joe. You should not be ashamed. You did your time with that lunatic. We thank God that he never hurt you or sold you during one of his anger filled rampages. You cannot blame yourself for his crimes. You're better without him. His death was a good thing."

Mattie, Lucy and I hugged her tightly and wished there was something else we could do. I wanted her to cry. I wanted her to be surprised so Sylvia would not think she knew anything about his death.

Boo held on to us for some time and then, pulling away from us she said, "I will be fine with this. I will feel better every minute that passes and I will help Victor in any way to get Joe's information. When we left for our trip I hated him for what he did to me. Now, I hate him for what he has done to so many others and I do not feel badly about his death. Forgive me for not crying, but I feel good that he is gone and I wish he would have been alive when he burned. If I knew he was doing that while married to me I would have turned him in to the police."

We all looked at her and then felt a deep peace. We did not know what to expect from Boo while Sylvia was telling her of the latest developments, but we were relieved by the way she handled the news. We were happy to have her in our life.

"I think it's time to start dressing like the new people we have become," I said, wondering what the future would bring.

Mattie and Lucy went to Boo and asked if she would join us in the dressing room for a makeover. She wrapped her arms around them and headed for the rooms where we met Sylvia just three days ago, the rooms where Sylvia had helped us through those first hours in Las Vegas.

"If anyone needs a makeover," Boo said, "it's me, mental and physical."

We laughed as only women in this situation could laugh; the laughter of freedom, of friendship, of harmony in our lives. Somehow we had gotten to this point in three short days.

Ricky, Juan and Phillip arrived in the lobby at 10:00 o'clock sharp. Garcia, having arrived fifteen minutes early, had been patiently waiting for them so he could escort them to Victor's penthouse on an unmarked floor which could only be accessed via elevator with a special security key.

Stepping off the elevator, into the penthouse space, they faced one another, looking amazed at the surroundings.

"Great place," Ricky said.

Phillip reached out and took Victor's hand shaking it as if they were old friends.

"I felt so bad for the girls their first night in Las Vegas with total strangers, perhaps confined to a small space with no food or water and probably at the mercy of some low life perverts who might be abusing them," Phillip said with a smile.

"Well, it could have happened had Danni and Josh not been the first to notice them in all their finery," Victor laughed.

There were tables set up for cards and tables for food. Linen table clothes, gold and white china, crystal stemware, pink napkins and floral arrangements covered the surfaces. Vanilla scented candles flickered in mirrors behind the bar mimicking a night scene of the city horizon.

"How many floors do you have here Victor?" Juan asked.

"We have three floors accommodating almost any need. There is a gym, a spa, on-line areas for computer work, dressing areas, clothes closets full of women's clothes, anything a woman could possibly imagine or want."

Josh and Danni had just come out of an area which we assumed to be their private quarters.

"Nice to see you," everyone said to one another.

Shawn would be arriving shortly. His presence would complete the number of players needed for a couple of poker tables.

Off to the right in an alcove filled with flowers was Sylvia, beautifully propped up on a chaise with a happy smile on her face.

"My God you look beautiful Sylvia," Ricky said.

"It is hard to look bad in this home. We have everything we need without leaving the premises," she said. "The girls should be with us in just a moment. This will be their last opportunity to select some more of the fabulous clothes they fell in love with over the last couple of days. I am so happy to have met them and have them as part of my life. They are wonderful women."

"Victor, I told Boo about Joseph. She was devastated to learn of the lives he ruined and surprised by his profession. Sorrow at Joe's passing was not warranted. She is anxious to help you find whatever files you are looking for at her home. I don't want her feeling responsible for his behavior. She feels she was blind to so much about him."

"Well, when they get out here we will toast to our future, now all of which should be good," Victor said.

The caterers brought out more lavish trays of food for the buffet and a special cake with Victor and Sylvia's name on top.

From the opposite side of the living area Lucy, Mattie and I entered to be with the others.

"My God," Ricky said, "are these the same trashy looking girls that scared the pawn shop owner out of his wits?"

"I think we need to take you back there," Phillip suggested, "and show him that you really weren't the whores he said you were. Maybe even buy a little trinket from him, something that would make you remember this weekend!"

"He's probably taking some time off," Juan said. "I think you frightened him Ricky telling him you would come back to kill him or worse."

"Kill him?" I said. "Did he call you names too?"

"No, no. I told him if you ladies were harmed, I would do the same to him!"

"We still need to return his phone," Phillip said.

"Why do you have his phone? Is it the phone that we sold for ten dollars?" Mattie questioned.

"He showed us how the whores looked from a picture on the phone," Phillip said with a smile on his face.

"Oh my goodness," Mattie said. "I hoped that would never be seen. If ever I run for public office that will probably show up in the Enquirer or some trash magazine!"

We girls had chosen black for our parting day. We wore black tops, black pants and black sandals. Coincidently, the men arrived in black shirts or tees and jeans. I thought we looked like a cult!

Mattie and Phillip went to the bar to get tall pink drinks.

Juan and Lucy went to talk to Victor. I glanced at the table and saw the cake showing Victor and Sylvia's name. I poked Ricky's side and pointed to the table.

He looked at me and shrugged. Sylvia did not see the cake yet.

Danni and Josh were over at Sylvia's chaise talking to her while Victor was having the caterer line up tall stemmed crystal glasses on the table.

I loved it here. I don't think I would have ever left if this was where I started out. The girls who worked for Victor's family had a very nice life. Ricky had told me that the girls Garcia took care of were treated wonderfully. They were provided first class education and were proud to be part of his family. I thought of these new acquaintances as "ladies of the night, not prostitutes". It was a family business where everyone was a happy participant.

Shawn had just come into the room from the elevator and now everyone who was coming was here. Shawn had a package for Victor which he gave to him at the bar.

Victor came to the library door and asked that we all come to where Sylvia was situated and join in a toast. The caterers brought glasses of champagne to each of us. They wheeled in the cake to be in front of Sylvia.

Victor raised his glass, and started his toast. "It has been thirteen years since Sylvia took over my house and my heart. She has been with me every step of the way and watched my business as if it were her own. She had asked only that I remain safe and keep my boys safe. She had asked that I not waste time on the low life of the city and that our family remain a proud family and one that others would consider a good example of honesty. I think I have honored her wish and for so long I thought I could protect her from the world. Last night when I thought I had almost lost her I realized how great the loss would be to me and my family. Well, I am asking Sylvia to honor me by becoming my wife and allowing me to take care of her for the rest of my life. I promise not to subject you, Sylvia, to anymore danger and I will keep you on a pedestal forever."

Sylvia was smiling and her face was completely flushed. She could not get up but she held out her arms to Victor. He came to her and sat on the chaise beside her. She put her hands on his face and said simply "Yes."

"I am the luckiest man in the world today," Victor said. "We will have the wedding when Sylvia is strong, hopefully in a month's time. Then I think we'll honeymoon in France. Sylvia has told me in the past she would like to visit the southern coast of France and this is a great time to make all her wishes come true. All of you will, of course, join us for the wedding and any that want to tag along to France would be more than welcome." He then produced the ring that Shawn had picked up from the jeweler that morning.

Sylvia held her breath as she gazed at the ring Victor placed on her finger. Tears formed in her eyes and she suddenly found it difficult to swallow as her cheeks flushed. She delicately extended her hand to Victor who took it to his lips and tenderly kissed it for several seconds.

My eyes were also wet with salty tears and I looked around the room to see that I was not alone in my emotions.

Everyone raised their glasses and drank to the new bride and groom.

Victor continued to toast. "I thank my new friends who came to Las Vegas for a vacation and accidently found us. I hope their futures will include us forever." All the glasses were raised.

"How very beautiful," I said to Mattie. "They are so in love. Look at Sylvia smiling at Josh and Danni. They seem to love her as much as their father. It's so wonderful!"

"This weekend has been so much better than I ever dreamed," said Lucy. "I could not have planned this much excitement. As vacations go, this was a ten!"

We ate too much and drank plenty of sweet late harvest Riesling watching the men playing cards. There was music playing from a sound system somewhere in the building and I was lightheaded from watching Ricky.

Baby was lying beside Sylvia and making sure her head was just exactly where Sylvia's long fingers could rest and pat her lightly.

Sylvia shared thoughts about the wedding dress she would design for her wedding. She had a favorite seamstress in Vegas and the dress would become a true labor of love. Everything would be soft pink, her dress and her traveling clothes, her accessory jewelry, and her night wear. She wanted everything to go with her wedding ring. It was such a perfect contrast to her dark skin. Victor would be so proud with her by his side. They completed each other.

I knew this special celebration was getting close to ending and I was wondering how we would get home. So far we had not talked about transportation.

"What shall we do for a car?" I asked as we sat together.

"You will fly," Victor said. "Actually Danni and Josh will fly you home and go to Boo's to get whatever files she can find. Then they'll bring Boo back here for her stay with Sylvia as she has generously offered to help with wedding arrangements."

"I'm looking forward to that," Boo said. "I don't want to be at home. There will be bad memories I am sure. I'll sell the house as soon as possible. Will there be a death certificate issued from Nevada?"

"Yes," Ricky said, trying to ease the pain of questions about Joseph.

"Then it's settled," Victor said.

As Ricky closed in beside me at the bar I could feel the warmth from his body all down my side.

"Do you suppose I could get your pertinent information before leaving? I would very much enjoy driving to San Diego to see you early in the week," Ricky said.

"I was hoping you would ask," I said. It's been a few years since I felt like entertaining a gentleman. I thought I would stalk you if you did not ask."

"Well I did not say I was a gentleman, but we will see if that's the final verdict," he laughed squeezing my hand at my side.

I could hardly wait, I thought. He felt like an old friend already, so I wouldn't have to waste much time with preliminaries. And he loved animals. He had a good soul.

Juan had asked Lucy to drive home with him, which delighted her. He would rent a car in Vegas and that would give them more time to talk about themselves. Also they could stop in Primm and get any luggage that was left in the room on our hasty departure. They were both rather shy, but not so with each other, talking non-stop when they were together in Vegas. There were no children and no baggage between them. I hoped Lucy had found a soul mate.

Mattie was showing Phillip the gym downstairs. They were both so physical and probably showing off to one another on one of the machines right now. Mattie, however, was dressed in a killer black blouse and slacks that would prevent her from contorting into too many special positions.

There had been so much activity since Sylvia came home. She and Victor needed some time just to appreciate and enjoy each other's company.

After all of our good-byes and hugs and kisses we gathered in the lobby and were ready to fly home by four o'clock.

One of Victor's men had taken Baby for a walk so she would be ready for her flight to her new home. Josh and Danni carried some luggage, which we felt might be guns, to the car outside. Mattie and I had no luggage, just a garment bag each. We actually did not even have our own make-up, but Sylvia made certain we had make-up and clothes in lovely little overnight bags as a reminder of the perfect trip. Boo took a large empty suitcase so she could bring back personal items when she returned. Lucy would be leaving in about another hour when Juan picked her up, so she took another outfit, just in case she spent the night at Juan's. She took some bath essentials and some alluring lingerie on the insistence of the girls living here.

We had our purses, but no licenses for driving, just a couple hair brushes and two credit cards, thanks to Ricky, Phillip and Juan checking our room at Primm.

Shawn saw us off at the airport and gave Joe's official death certificate to Boo for safekeeping. She would need that to sell their joint property and to settle any estate he may have had. She thanked Shawn for all his quiet support and then gave him a tender hug. She started to choke up as she apologized for all the damage Joe had done in his life and hoped they could still be friends. Shawn was surprised that she would even think they could not be friends and told her so.

"You're a fine person Boo and you should feel no responsibility for the dark path your husband chose. The world is a better place without him," Shawn assured her.

We boarded the Cessna with Baby in tow and were off the ground in less than ten minutes. Our flight plan would land us at a small regional airport just north of San Diego named Palomar in a little over an hour. Hoping to minimize any further hassles and delays, we would be arriving at a private hangar belonging to a friend of Victors, which would mean no inspection of the mysterious luggage Josh and Danni were bringing along with them.

Once airborne we anticipated few problems, until we began to feel rocky turbulence and saw massive thunderclouds, lightning flashes and rain squalls over Death Valley approaching quickly. The storm completely engulfed the southern sky from ground level to over twenty-five thousand feet, well above our ceiling limit. The only course of action was to divert our flight path to the northern stretch of the Mojave where clear skies still prevailed and storm dangers could be avoided. This circuitous route to Palomar added another forty minutes to our flight and we were all antsy to empty our bladders and get to Boo's place as quickly as possible when we touched down.

Josh demonstrated his fast thinking skills and called Enterprise Car Rental at Palomar while we were still airborne, arranging for a full size car to be ready for us when we arrived and thereby saving us at least a few minutes of additional delay.

Fulfilling their "Service is Job One" slogan, an Enterprise agent was awaiting our arrival at the hangar with a blue Lincoln Town Car. We hit the restrooms in the hangar and then quickly loaded Baby and the luggage. The Town Car's extra legroom was a welcome relief after the almost two hour flight in the cramped Cessna. Our creature comfort delights were quickly dismissed as we redirected our attention to the goal of reaching Boo's home so that Josh and Danni could get the business side of the trip out of the way.

As we pulled into Boo's driveway we passed an old van without identification or signage on the vehicle leaving rather quickly. "Probably a delivery," Danni said.

"Usually there would be a company name on the vehicle if that was the case," Boo replied.

It had been less than twenty four hours since Manny and Benjamin's man were summarily dumped from the plane and it did not seem possible that news of the event could have traveled quickly enough to allow an interception of our arrival, but the presence of the van on this otherwise quiet street spooked us all..

Parking directly in front of the house allowed quick access to the front door where it was immediately obvious that someone else had gotten to the house before we arrived. We noticed from the car that the front door was wide open. Josh approached the opened door while Danni circled around to the back of the house after giving us specific instructions to remain in the car until he signaled an all clear.

"Gads," Boo said as she peered into the house. Even from the town car she could see that everything was upside down and torn apart. The beautiful down cushions had apparently been ripped up by the intruders and feathers were still flying around the house, blowing out the front door and landing on everything in sight.

Boo was trying to be unfazed about the destruction, adopting the same Zen like calm she had displayed during our previous weekend's adventures when faced with similar threatening situations. She wore a look of bad memories.

I looked at her and smiled. "What you did is over and I for one don't blame you and will never say a word about it. No one, Boo, would find fault with what happened. I think it is best that we just find Joe's records and get on with life. We can buy lots of new pillows."

It was at that point that Boo's composure began to deteriorate as she hugged me and started to cry. Boo had never had a real friend to confide in other than her parents and her realization that she now had several true friends who genuinely cared about her welfare produced a sudden flood of tears. Mattie saw what was happening and came over to hug us both. Rubbing Boo's back she predicted, "Boo will be fine when she gets out of here and back with Sylvia."

Josh and Danni came out on the front porch after carefully checking out the entire house for intruders.

"It's clear, no one stayed back to watch for us. It looks like they didn't have a clue as to where his computer or records were hidden," Danni said. "They did a pretty good job of looking everywhere. We were probably lucky to have encountered that storm or we would have been here in the middle of their ransacking the house."

"Not everywhere," Boo said. "He worked in a room behind the garage that you can only get to from inside the garage. The door is concealed behind a tall tool cabinet. That's where he kept his "clients" records safe. He would say, "just in case of fire they should be stored safely behind the metal cabinets.""

We moved into the garage and Boo pushed aside the tool cabinet, exposing the hidden access to the office. Through the door was what appeared to be a fully furnished office, complete with a student size desk, two computers, a four drawer filing cabinet and a safe that was much too heavy for two men to lift. How the clunky safe had actually been moved into the hidden office was a complete mystery.

"Victor will be delighted with this information," Josh said.

"Where is the suitcase Danni?" Josh asked.

Danni lifted the suitcase to a table and removed a small plastic explosive device that he carefully taped to the handle of the safe.

"Now, if you ladies would be so kind as to leave this room, we will see if we have enough explosive to open that box," Danni said.

Fearing the worst, we all headed out to presumed safety in the back yard while Josh wired up a detonator pin and rigged a remote firing trigger. He joined us with a wide grin and dialed up the explosive trigger code on his cell phone. We covered our ears in anticipation of what was to follow.

A muffled roar boomed from the garage followed by clouds of dust and debris. The wall between the garage and the office collapsed from the shock of the blast followed by the sound of hand and power tools, paint cans and all manner of assorted hardware crashing to the garage floor from the wall cabinets that had previously held them in fine order.

"Wow!" I said. "What if that gizmo would have detonated in the plane?"

"Well, bottom line, we would have had a sudden and unscheduled landing and most likely wouldn't be here to talk about it right now," laughed Josh, causing us all to raise eyebrows and grimace.

As we entered the garage we were more than surprised to see twenty dollar bills floating in the air, slowly settling on the debris field that was just moments before a functional office. There were several accounting journals with red covers on the floor along with a number of sealed plastic wrappers of pictures and passports. There was little doubt that among this newly uncovered treasure trove of documents would be the highly sought after information Manny's men would have killed to get their filthy hands on.

We gathered up all the bits and pieces as fast as we could and Josh and Danni took what was left of the two computers, all the safe's contents and the scorched files from the four drawer filing cabinet out to the car for safe keeping.

Boo grabbed a framed picture of herself lying on the cluttered floor, still intact, apparently taken while on vacation in Hawaii. Joe must have thought about her while he was selling other women. How touchingly sentimental I thought, but did not say a word.

Josh and Danni filled an empty suitcase and two storage boxes they found in the garage with the salvageable papers and suggested that we all go directly to the Palomar airstrip to exchange the car. This seemed like a smart plan of action given the unknown whereabouts of the recent intruders at Boo's house and Mattie and I immediately agreed. If there was anyone following us we certainty would prefer to avoid what would likely turn out to be an unpleasant encounter.

We headed back to airport hangar with Boo's one stuffed suitcase containing personal items and Danni and Josh's boxes and miscellaneous components. Danni dropped us all at the hangar and headed to the terminal Enterprise office to return the car. With somewhat questionable judgment considering our stated intent to maintain a low key presence he then showed up at the hangar ten minutes later with a red Boss Mustang convertible sporting a huge white racing strip down the hood and trunk. "Enjoy the ride for a week," he said, apparently believing he was giving us a special parting gift to help remember our colorful weekend adventure.

The Cessna had been refueled while Danni dealt with the car and was prepped for departure when he arrived back. Josh, Danni and Boo quickly stowed the suitcase containing all of Joe's records and Boo's personal suitcase in the hold and boarded the aircraft. Looking out the plane's windows they flashed large smiles and thumbs up. With the hatch now closed we watched the plane taxi off onto the runway in anticipation of a speedy take-off clearance.

Josh and Danni had hit a potential bonanza of incriminating files in Joe's garage and were eager to cull through them in search of evidence that would lead to the prosecution of several so called "upstanding public servants" that were thought to be heavily involved in the illegal smuggling network. Here was the smoking gun of criminal conspiracy that Victor, Shawn and Garcia had needed to make their case.

There would be the usual protestations of innocence, denials of involvement and claims of harassment from the aggrieved suspects but the documents now in hand provided a clear paper trail of money transfers and payments that would allow authorities to mete out harsh justice for the many co-conspirators of the long running and far reaching smuggling scheme that had spawned so much misery.

"What a day!" I said.

"That was more like five days in one!" Mattie corrected me as we buckled up in the Mustang and headed home.

"What do you think Mattie? Want to make a pit stop at Starbucks?" I said, secretly hoping she didn't want to dally.

"I don't think so," she said. "Some nice chilled Riesling and a long soak in a warm tub sound more like what I really need now."

As we drove towards the coast and the setting sun Baby relished the open air in the back seat as only dogs can do. She had a safe new home only a few minutes away and I could see her smiling face filling the rear view mirror. I couldn't contain a laugh as I noticed the wind had exaggerated her lips to appear that she'd had silicone implants, thereby resembling a certain once famous Hollywood bimbo who'd gone overboard with the big lips thing and subsequently, and unhappily, been dubbed "Slug Lips" in the tabloids.

My planned weekend of rest and relaxation with Mattie, Lucy and Boo had taken several crazy U turns and detours during the past seventy-two hours. Amazingly, we had survived fate's booby-traps unscathed and, all things considered, had most likely improved our ability to deal with challenging future surprises. Although I'd expended enough nervous energy over the weekend to cover multiple bungee jumps off Victoria Falls and I badly needed about twelve hours of undisturbed sleep to recharge my batteries, I was exhilarated and strangely energized by the prospects of a new life with Baby and maybe my real Cowboy.

I was thinking I might actually write a book about this most memorable weekend adventure and the strange characters I had encountered along the way, both living and deceased.

But first, there was a wedding to plan.

**The Start of New Beginnings**